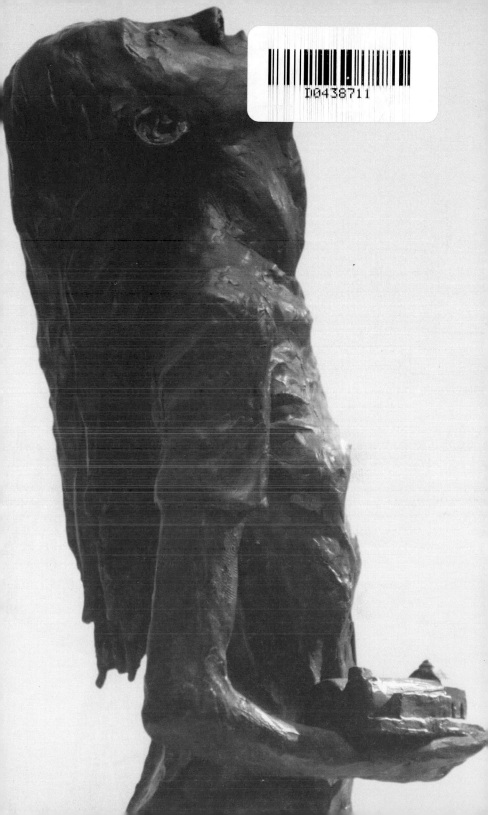

Alva & Irva

Also by Edward Carey

Observatory Mansions

EDWARD CAREY

Alva & Irva

The Twins who Saved a City

PICADOR

First published 2003 by Picador
an imprint of Pan Macmillan Ltd
Pan Macmillan, 20 New Wharf Road, London NI 9RR
Basingstoke and Oxford
Associated companies throughout the world
www.panmacmillan.com

ISBN 0 330 41321 X

Grateful acknowledgement is made to the following for permission to
reprint previously published material: extract from *The Complete Poems of Cavafy*
by Constantine Cavafy (trans. Rae Dalven) reprinted by permission of
Harcourt Publishers Ltd Trade Division.

Printed and bound in Great Britain by
Mackays of Chatham plc, Chatham, Kent

For Elizabeth

Acknowledgements

Craig Czury, Joe and Renata Gayon, Ariel Kotker, Tom Langdon, Anna Searle, Gabija Veberiene, Jeremy Wellens, Claudia Woolgar and Maria-Cecilia Woolgar have helped me in varying ways through the slow process of this book, by taking me on visits to ruined collieries, by providing me with places to write; by daily sending me postcards of the same city, by keeping still in unpleasant positions for many long hours, by taking photographs of teeny-weeny buildings. I would like to give particular thanks to the ever-patient and generous Janos Stone, who nannied me through what was I'm sure for him the exhausting sculpture part of this project, and to Isobel Dixon, Ursula Doyle, Elizabeth McCracken, Richard Milner and, most hugely, Ann Patty for their wonderful advice on how I might proceed with the writing part of it.

You will find no new lands, you will find no other seas.
The city will follow you. You will roam the same
streets. And you will age in the same neighbourhoods;
and you will grow gray in these same houses.

Always you will arrive in this city. Do not hope for any other –
There is no ship for you, there is no road.
As you have destroyed your life here
in this little corner, you have ruined it in the entire world.

C. P. Cavafy

CENTRAL ENTRALLA

① Bekstis Lubatkinas, Lubatkin's Tower
② Cathedral
③ Baptistry
④ Bell Tower
⑤ City Hall
⑥ Central Post Office
⑦ Opera House
⑧ Namos Tectonijas, Tectonic House
⑨ Civic Theatre
⑩ Police Central Office
⑪ Namos Sirkinos, Sirkin House
⑫ Entralla Zoo
⑬ Entralla Art Museum
⑭ Lubatkin Statue
⑮ Le Grand Lubatkin
⑯ Entralla University
⑰ Alva & Irva Dapps Memorial
⑱ St Onne's Church
⑲ International World Hotel
⑳ Central Library
㉑ Pig Mikel's Tattoo Parlour
㉒ Café Louis
㉓ Kvardos Panas, Bread Square
㉔ Pulvin Street School
㉕ 42 Pult Street
㉖ Television Tower
㉗ Central Train Station
● Trolley Bus Stop

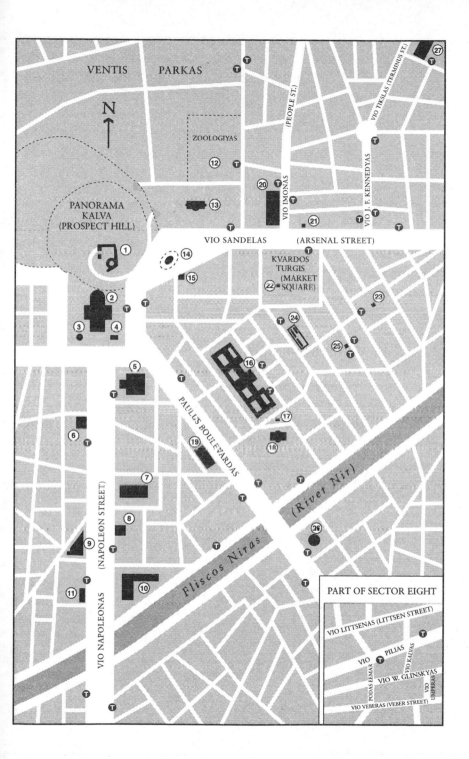

Welcome to the History of Alva & Irva, the Twins who Saved a City

A New Statue for Our City

There were once twin sisters in our city trapped in a loneliness that was perpetually crowded by each other. One day, in a desperate urge to fit in, in a deep yearning to belong somewhere, these sisters decided to map our city, to make a detailed inventory of our home, to make precise miniature models of every street, of every dwelling. One twin stayed at home constructing this ever swelling model, built out of plasticine purchased from a toy shop on Pilias Street, the other walked the city, day and night, gathering up all the details, armed only with a notebook and a tape measure. For many years they kept to their task and in the end, I think, they were the greatest of experts on this city of ours, this city of Entralla, that will perhaps ever be known. Now, throughout Entralla, in our schools, in our work places, in our many homes, people talk of them constantly.

Due to the absolute harmony of its location, crowned with its magnificent ruined fortress, its marvellous churches and excellently constructed secular buildings, Entralla offers priceless treasures for any sensitive visitor. Location, architecture and time, as if three great friends, have conspired to create a masterpiece. If the city, the opposite of nature, is the pinnacle of man's achievements, then this city, as I am sure you will agree once you have had a chance to peruse it, may represent a supreme example from which many another city's beauty may be judged.

Though it must be admitted: Entralla, through some spite of fate, is not a famous city. Yet it is ours and we are proud of it. Somehow you have come to us and you are welcome. Look about you, see churches, cunningly restored, of Gothic, Renaissance, Baroque and classical architecture; the clues to the twins' lives lie all about the city, in the buildings, in the inhabitants. So see people now, our people, overfed and underfed, ripe and stale. See our city moving urgently and sedentarily about its business. Welcome and look about you please. Throughout Entralla there are various statues of people, busts or full length, in metal or in stone. Foreigners may look at these statues and wonder whom they represent, for all the proud faces will mean nothing to them. These sculptures are the famous people of Entralla. Their names are irrelevant to all the other peoples of the world, their times and deeds remain obscure, there are no books published to explain who they are and why they have been thought worthy of commemoration. They are not mentioned in the official guidebook to Entralla which, though available in one book store only, is published in five of the more popular languages of the world. But it is only thirty pages long. And it must seem to our few foreign visitors that our sculptures and monuments represent a little people of no worldly importance, as if our city were only a village and that we had chosen to immortalise local characters, such as typically can be found in a village – the priest, the mayor, the fat butcher, the idiot. But Entralla is a city and not a village.

As the world is daily shrunk by technology it has finally been decided that one history should be made available to a larger public. It has also been decided that I, August Hirkus, a slightly balding man in my fifties, neither thin nor fat, with little about me that might attract attention, a man whom people may even describe as possessing plain or bland features, that I should write the introduction and various other passages to this history since I knew many of the people concerned and since I went to live abroad some years ago, and returned with a knowledge of the English language – that language which is supposedly the most popular in the world – so that I might translate this history into this popular English language, thereby allowing as many people as possible to learn it.

Of course some foreigners will say, 'You are wrong, there are at least two concrete incidents when your city made international

4

news.' This knowledgeable foreigner would boast that the name of Entralla was certainly familiar to him and that he had even seen brief shots of the city on television. Such people are few, such people are precious. It is true that Entralla suffered from an earthquake some years ago and much damage was inflicted upon it. And for a while afterwards many foreign visitors came, but these visitors were businessmen and business-women who showed interest only in repairing our city, and in repairing it as they saw fit. They have all gone now.

The other concrete incident that occurred in Entralla which may have been heard of abroad, was reported on many of the lunchtime television news shows across the world, but was unfortunately not to be found on the evening news; by then a war had broken out somewhere which had succeeded in ending the lives of fifty-two people and in halving a moment of fame for us. This incident is perhaps one which many people from Entralla would rather not have had broadcast at all, for it is not likely to improve the world's impression of us; rather, in fact, the reverse. In this incident, which is still talked about now, a woman died of a heart attack whilst on a trolley bus but the trolley bus driver refused to stop the bus until his route had been completed; he had orders, he said, and they could not be disobeyed. So the dead woman remained on the trolley bus until it had journeyed several circuits around the city and finally returned to the trolley bus station. Little did the passengers that day know that this journey was to become one of the two concrete incidents for which Entralla may be internationally known. Little did the dead woman know that her journey on the trolley bus would be her last and that her death would become, briefly, world news. Little did the bus driver, a certain Andrius Chapin, know that his refusal to stop the trolley bus with the dead body inside it would result in his becoming, briefly, internationally famous, and locally famous for ever. Now whenever he gives his name, at a party or at some public meeting or other, people always ask him, 'Weren't you the trolley bus driver who refused to stop the trolley bus with the dead body *inside it?' And Andrius Chapin always begrudgingly says, 'Yes', and the person who met him goes home that night and tells his incredulous family that he has actually shaken hands with the former trolley bus driver who had refused to stop the trolley bus with the dead woman inside it. This incident made the news because the world apparently found it shocking. A person dying in this way touched their imagination, they have buses too and they feared for themselves. There was something extraordinarily riveting and comprehensible about an individual dying in a bus and being driven in circles around a city, unable to get off; it was far easier to understand, for example, than thousands of lives ended in an earthquake. In Entralla, however, most people found the news tragi-comic; in fact, many people still find the incident amusing today, and such fun has been had from it that there was even a story going around that a statue would be made of the trolley bus driver or that the trolley bus in which the dead woman had sat for three hours without being removed would be exhibited in the main hall of our principal art gallery. Such stories are mere mischief-making. Certainly no one is going to make a statue of the trolley bus driver. But, as fate would have it, a statue is to be made of the woman who died in the trolley bus. The reason for this statue is not to form a permanent reminder of the lamentable death of this woman but as a celebration of her life. For us, the residents of our city, the incident inside the trolley bus was made doubly appalling or amusing, depending on your viewpoint, because the woman who died on the bus was indeed a famous person from Entralla and the international media refused to refer to her in any terms except for 'the dead woman'. For them only her death was significant. For us her life was of enormous importance and her death, at the young age of thirty-four, was unworthy of her. The dead woman was one of the twin sisters, one half of Alva and Irva.*

The publication of this story, in English, is timed to coincide with the unveiling of a statue, in one of our many city squares, of the dead woman from the trolley bus and of her sister. At their feet, also to be sculpted in clay and cast in bronze, will be a model in miniature of the central portion of Entralla, that portion which holds our most significant pieces of architecture.

So soon, when our precious foreigners come to visit they will see this new statue and wonder if these two young women, Alva and Irva, were Entralla's version of the more famous twins Romulus and Remus, founders of the city of Rome, capital of Italy. We would smile at this suggestion, but, without commenting directly on it, steer the foreigners – or perhaps I should say foreigner, it is best not to be too optimistic – in the direction of the university bookshop where a history of the twins – written principally by Alva, the eldest of the twins (but with added interjections by myself, which will always incidentally appear in italic type) – can be found, in English, at a very reasonable price.

For the convenience of our foreign visitors – most of whom, it has been noticed, stay in Entralla for a mere twenty-four hours (some for considerably less) – breaks have been included in this volume, labelled Interludes, one for morning coffee, one for lunch, one for supper – which have been listed in chronological order for the sake of neatness, but can of course be taken whenever required. Please note that at some restaurants and cafés a reduction of 10 per cent will be given to customers carrying this book. However, should the visitor have longer than one day in which to enjoy the various entertainments Entralla has to offer, please feel free to read this book at whatever pace seems attractive. So welcome. Welcome indeed.

Part One

DALLIA & LINAS

A Love Story in Our Central Post Office

The Central Post Office

The Central Post Office of Entralla can be found at 8–10 Napoleon Street, hours Monday to Friday 9 a.m.–5 p.m., Saturday 10 a.m.–12 p.m., closed Sundays. It is a large cube of a building, two storeys high, notable only for its fake marble cladding and its four Corinthian columns in the entrance portico – added at a much later date than the building's original construction, and certainly

The Central Post Office

without the architect's permission. Together these features lend the vague impression of a classical temple, and perhaps it might initially be considered our city's minor version of the Acropolis of Athens were it not for the fact that the building is so caked in filth (soot, bird excrement, vehicle exhaust, industrial grime) that its neglect gives it away for what it is: an ordinary public service building. Abused, ugly, useful.

★ ★ ★

The older buildings on Napoleon Street are like parents to the newer ones. Parents are the beginning, without our parents where would we be? We may not like to think of them in the carnal act, but surely they were at it. Otherwise we should not have happened. Their energy, their youthful exchanges, created us. Before my sister Irva and I there were Dallia and Linas.

We like to think our parents are as vital as buildings to the existence of Entralla. Everybody should be permanently reminded of them. There should be a big sign, just so everyone can know, 'On this step Dallia and Linas made love.' For their energies one night on the top step of Central Post Office was the essential first act in our lives. It was not merely the quiet grunting of two employees of the post office – for so Mother and Father were – but the call of something far grander and more significant. How can I explain the magnitude of their physical act? I'm not sure. But now, after a few moments thought, perhaps I have it. Down Napoleon Street is Cathedral Square, and in the square, as well as the cathedral, are two other buildings: the bell tower and the baptistry. The bell tower, and there's nothing exceptional in this, is tall and thin. The baptistry, and this is unexceptional news too, is short and fat. I think of Father and Mother. I think of the bell tower and the baptistry.

The bell tower looks down and loves the squat baptistry, the baptistry looks up and loves the beanpole bell tower. Now let me cast these buildings in the forthcoming event. Let me label the bell tower Linas-father, for if he was a building rather than a person he would indeed have been a tall, gangly type of structure. And let me label the baptistry Dallia-mother, for were she to be built out of limestone, she too would be only one storey in height, and she too would spread herself out in a horizontal fashion. So now, lower the light of day into a more romantic atmosphere, turn on the moon, and see the beginnings of us, of Alva and of Irva. Hear a faint rumbling as the bell tower pulls himself from his foundations in Cathedral Square, and lays himself down on top of the baptistry. And as the city vibrates with this act of love, to the happy groans of the bell tower and the baptistry: we begin. That's how it should have been marked, not by a little panting from two adolescents on the top entrance step of a building, but by the loud ecstatic bellowing of great architecture as it bangs away, building against building.

Down Napoleon Street, all those years ago, before the Benetton shop arrived, before the electric green crosses of the pharmacies flashed on and off, perhaps even before the advent of colour, yes, years ago when the world was black and white, was a time before Irva and I, a time when our father met our mother.

Father's was not a happy beginning. Weak and dreamy orphan Linas Dapps, so the records state, was found one morning in the porch of the convent of Saint Inga on the outskirts of the city – in exactly the same manner as fifty or so other babies are found each year. The nun who found the baby named him Linas because Linas had been the name of her lover, who had loved her and spurned her but whom she had continued to love and who was the reason for her voluntary incarceration. She also named him Dapps, which of course is our name too; and also many other people's name. Dapps is the most common surname in our country, it's like Smith in Britain, Müller in Germany, Popescu in Romania, Suzuki in Japan. This nun must have wanted Father to fit in, to be anonymous in a crowd, to be just another person, just another Dapps. And so with these two names Linas Dapps, our father (long dead sadly), was sent out into the world. And it was these two names – signifying an earnest, nervous and tall man with a large head – that the postmaster was obliged, by certain civic authorities, to employ in the post office.

Dallia Grett, that's Mother, worked behind post office counter number twelve. She was very young to work behind a counter, only nearing the end of her seventeenth year, and this made her early life at work somewhat strained. Some of the other workers were jealous and made unconvincing attempts to hide their jealousy. This meant that Mother had no friends at work and loathed the long day's toil there. She had been rewarded this job, as she was acutely aware, not by merit but simply because her father, our grandfather (sadly he's no longer either), was the postmaster of our city and had decided, without consulting his daughter, that as soon as he could get away with it he would employ her in the post office. Grandfather was a frugal man and had determined, without consulting his wife, our grandmother (a bit part if ever there was one, long-long ago snuffed out), that he would have only one child. He was sure in his mind that his progeny would be male and would in turn become the next postmaster, and the moment Grandmother was confirmed pregnant he immediately ceased his nocturnal pokings. But fate is cruel, Grandmother's efforts at bringing a life into this world proved too much for her (goodbye, Grandmother, sorry I never knew you), and it was with such a sad heart that Grandfather lifted the wriggling female lump from his stationary wife's bedside in the hospital ward. He peeked between the tiny, plump legs. He sighed. No, there could be no confusion. A little slit. A girl.

But Grandfather soon cheered up (always an onwards-onwards sort of man our grandfather): an idea had come to him, and the idea made him smile. Grandfather was not a man of many ideas, and generally he did not trust such extravagances, but this idea, it seemed to him, was a good one. His daughter would be employed, at the earliest possible opportunity, in the post office, and once inside the post office he was sure that this daughter of his would trap a sensible young man and that sensible young man would be sure to marry his daughter and become in time our city's next postmaster. A son-in-law as postmaster was an acceptable compromise. That was the idea, and he was so pleased with it that it had scarcely altered when he sent his daughter to work at the age of sixteen, with a smile on his face. But Grandfather didn't notice, as the sixteen years crept slowly by, that no one was going to put a hot iron in the fire in order to brand Mother beautiful. Mother had uneven teeth, a large mole on her right cheek and freckles all over her face. The mole was roughly circular and Grandfather used often to comment that it was by some surely meaningful coincidence the exact shape of our city. In fact, its shape bore a remarkable similarity to that of the old city of Culemborg in the Netherlands, even though Culemborg is a city Mother never once visited.

Mother worked behind a post office counter, Father delivered letters, the post office was where they met and where they fell in love. I can boast no beautiful backdrop to their courtship; I will not pretend that the Central Post Office is or was in any way comparable to the Ponte Vecchio in Florence, Italy, where the great Dante fell in love with Beatrice. Rather, our post office was a large dusty hall, which no matter how often its floor was swept and mopped always somehow remained dusty, and remains dusty to this day. There were twelve counters – today there are thirty-two – and back then they were made of wood; today they are of metal and have glass divides between the office and hall. But customers wishing to thump a post-office assistant in the old times could feel free to do so without any let or hindrance. And this, in fact, did occasionally happen.

Grandfather considered the army of his employees, wondering which one his daughter would trap. Would it be Tomas, a fine boy but a little too headstrong? Or would it be Kurt, a bit fat perhaps, but undeniably a good sort? Or maybe Victor, serious and proud and never one to waste a moment of the post office's time? 'Dallia and Victor!,' Grandfather shrieked to himself in his bath one night, spilling the water over the sides. That was it, it was certain to be Victor. And in these delightful contemplations he never once considered the weak and dreamy orphan Linas.

But his daughter made little impression on either Tomas or Kurt. And Victor's mind was far too occupied ever to consider girls or courting; he was simply too busy, and if the female form did ever enter his consciousness it was only when illustrations of women appeared on stamps, and in these instances he simply distorted their image with the aid of the post office franking machine and they were immediately forgotten.

On the historic day Linas Dapps, our tall father, approached desk twelve, where our mother, our short and squat mother, worked, it was not love that was in his mind, but stamps. Some men love power, some men love women, some men love boys, some men love cars, some men love firearms, some men love matchstick buildings; well, Father was one of those men who love stamps, a small breed admittedly but a breed nevertheless. On the day he approached Mother he was concerned only to glimpse the new set of stamps that had just been issued and he knew that he would not be welcomed at any of the other counters. During his one and a half years at the post office he had slowly worked his way from counter one to counter twelve, bothering each of the workers in turn, pleading with them to show him a set of new stamps.

At first the employees behind the counters had tolerated him, even laughed at his demands – particularly Marta Stroud of number three, an unfortunate woman with a disease called psoriasis. No one else in the post office showed such enthusiasm for stamps. But after a time the yearning of this orphan boy had become tiring to them. They shunned him, they pushed him away, they complained that they were busy, that he would see the stamps in due course on his delivery rounds. This was true – soon Father would have as much time as he desired to linger over each new stamp as he went about the city, from house to house. But those stamps, Father would protest, had been franked; they were no longer the pure virgin stamps that could be found at the post office counters. Oh, he would sigh, there was something magical about those unused stamps arranged neatly in blocks, still with their serrated edges untorn and their glue unlicked. They were the nearest thing, he believed, to innocence. Father absolutely had to see the stamps on the first day of their issue, he had to be by them when they were first shown to the world, he had to make their acquaintance before the ink of the franking machines sullied them. But these post office clerks were harsh, principled people.

So Father came to Mother, and Mother did not send him away. He asked her politely if he might view the new set of stamps, and she, innocently, and despite the chuckling that could clearly be heard from all the other counters – particularly from Marta Stroud at number three – allowed him. Father bowed his large head over the new stamps, so that his nose was just millimetres from their surface; he carefully studied the complete pages of stamps one by one, with his eyes and with his fingers, sighing and purring all the while.

The stamps on this occasion were of various beetles.[1] It was the least pleasant set of stamps Mother had ever seen. When she first viewed the sheets of stamps, each holding a small beetle within perforated barriers, fifty beetles to a page, it did not take much imagination to see these beetles coming to life and scuttling and pattering beyond their perforated borders, away from the heavy stamp book in which they were all collected, infiltrating every inch of Mother's counter and even wandering, tickling in an uncomfortable way, onto Mother's person and going for an afternoon stroll beneath her clothes, about her skin. She did not

---

1. INCIDENTALLY – *National insects drawn by our very own artists of entomology.*

like these beetles, she was happy when someone bought a beetle and she could pick up her official rubber stamp and with great energy crush it in an inky and official death.

And yet this collection of beetle stamps, Mother noticed, was loved by Father. He practically inhaled them. And once he had finally finished introducing himself to this new set, he very sincerely thanked Mother and even asked if he could come again. She agreed. And from that day onwards he would always come to Mother at counter twelve as soon as his rounds were finished. At first of course he had to crouch by her, for there was supposed to be only one person behind each counter and accordingly only one seat was provided. After a week of aching limbs father brought a wooden stool with him which ever after lived side by side with Mother's plastic chair in the twelfth counter booth. Perhaps that plastic chair and that wooden stool were slowly falling in love too – they seemed somehow to belong to each other. Perhaps this abandoned child and this half-orphan were instinctively drawn together by a profound yearning for absent people. Perhaps each immediately felt the want that surrounded the other, and instantly closed ranks in desperation for a whole. But Mother would not tolerate Father just sitting beside her all day, silent and smiling. She offered Father various tasks. Would he, for example, frank the stamps with her official rubber stamp or take the envelopes over to the franking machine? 'No, no,' he said nervously, 'I couldn't do that.' Would he, for example, tear out the stamps for Mother to give to the customers? 'No, no,' he said beginning to sweat, 'I wouldn't do that.' Would he then be prepared to lick the stamps and stick them onto the envelopes for her? 'Yes,' he said at last, after much hesitation, 'I could certainly have a go at that.' And that was what he did. Father licked all Mother's stamps for her (generally, the Entrallan Post Office Lick, as it was known to the employees, did not involve the act of licking at all but consisted solely of passing the stamp over a damp sponge, thus ensuring that anything as unpleasantly personal as a tongue remained hidden at all times). And as Father's long pink tongue exposed itself in front of Mother, in front of the customers, Father imagined himself licking a tiny segment of Mother's skin, approximately one and a half centimetres by one centimetre, and Mother too imagined herself being licked. Minute by minute she would imagine different one-and-a-half-centimetres-by-one-centimetre portions of herself being licked by Father's large and, to her, irresistible tongue. At the end of the day she would believe that Father had licked every centimetre of skin on her sixteen-year-old body.

Unhappy Grandfather, the postmaster, began to see his plans take on grotesque shapes. Orphan Linas, that motherless, fatherless, rootless man, as postmaster? Weak and dreamy orphan Linas as his daughter's husband? Never! Generally he could combat his daughter's inappropriate infatuation by calling her away from the post office's granite steps where he would find her every evening sitting with Orphan Linas. But one night, some four months after Mother and Father had met, grandfather was unable to call Mother away because he was in the City Hall,[2] at the official annual meeting for principal workers of the post offices throughout our region.

So now I think again of the bell tower and the baptistry.

When Grandfather left the City Hall late that night, drunk and red-faced, he looked across Napoleon Street to the Central Post Office and saw, lying down, in the shadows, on the top step, two people in post office uniforms. His immediate reaction may have been to leave them alone in their happiness, in order, perhaps, to enjoy the delight of publicly embarrassing them the next

---

2. SITES OF INTEREST. The City Hall. *The Banqueting Hall, within the City Hall, with its magnificent painted ceiling, can be made available to tourists to view by polite enquiry at the porter's desk or may even be booked for business conferences at a very reasonable rate – regrettably, all five city hall porters speak no English.*

morning in front of the entire small army of his employees. But then he recognised his daughter.

I shan't tell of Grandfather's screams. I shan't tell of Mother's yells and tears. I shan't tell of the slap that Father received from Grandfather. I shan't tell of the swelling that immediately began to deform Father's face. I shan't tell of the hair-pulling and kicks that Mother delivered to Grandfather after the slap. I shan't tell of Grandfather sitting afterwards on a step crying like a five-year-old child. I shan't even tell of the miserable night of sleeplessness that occurred at Grandfather's residence. Nor shall I tell how things seemed scarcely better the morning afterwards. For these things are better left unsaid.

I shall tell that the following morning, as Grandfather climbed the post office steps to begin his day's work, he saw a pair of girl's panties abandoned near the entrance door. I shall tell that seeing those panties removed any remaining doubts in his mind. I shall tell that picking up those panties before anyone else had a chance to see them was the saddest thing that this man would ever do in his life. I shall tell that as this man hastily thrust his daughter's panties into his jacket pocket he began to die a little, and that his eyes would ever after see the world a little out of focus. I shall tell that a pair of panties in Grandfather's jacket pocket meant an end to all dreams he had previously had for the future of his post office. I shall also tell that panties in Grandfather's pocket meant that a marriage must be arranged. And I shall also tell that the marriage concerned one Dallia Grett and a certain weak and dreamy Linas Dapps.

A Newly Married Couple
Once Played Husband and Wife
on Napoleon Street

Napoleon Street

Napoleon Street, a major thoroughfare of our city, does not only extinguish itself into Cathedral Square, does not only contain our Central Post Office, but is home also to our Opera House and our Civic Theatre, and is perhaps the most cultivated street in our city. However, various other buildings with far less colourful

Napoleon Street, showing City Hall and Cathedral Square

purposes also operate there, among them Police Central Office and Tectonic House. The street is named after a certain celebrity of diminished stature who is rumoured to have entered our city once with his dishevelled and retreating army and even to have slept one night here, on the stage of our Opera House, where Wagner and Rossini and Mozart have passed so many nights. Historical evidence to support this has not yet been found, but the search has not been entirely abandoned, and we daily live in hope.

★ ★ ★

Dallia Grett became Dallia Dapps in the small chapel of Saint Piter Martyr's Church on the western side of Prospect Hill. Piter Martyr's Church no longer exists; it fell down several years ago.[3]

I try to picture Mother in her wedding dress, I try to picture Father standing next to her. I suppose Father must have been very nervous and probably stuttered until everybody wanted to say the words for him. And then I wonder how Grandfather reacted to the expansion of his daughter, already visible under the wedding dress, which the doctor had called 'Pregnancy'. If it was impossible to imagine Grandfather at his home on Pult Street it might be assumed that he had registered the fact of his daughter's metamorphosis only by the different way he addressed Father in the post office – no longer calling him 'Orphan Linas', but terming him instead 'Potent Linas'. But Grandfather can be imagined in this building in Pult Street, I can even picture Grandfather sitting in his study, because I know the room so well. I imagine Grand-

---

3. LOST TREASURES OF ENTRALLA. The Chapel of Saint Piter the Martyr. *There would be no reward for any excursion to this region of the city, either optional or mandatory. It is a small miracle that this church – a superb example of fifteenth-century Christian architecture – stood for so long, being, as it was, predominantly made of wood, wood that had housed within it a population of insects whose numbers could have rivalled any of the great and famous municipalities of the world.*

father at his desk back in those black and white days. I imagine him talking. Who are you talking to, Grandfather? To the ghost of Grandmother? No, Grandfather's talking to his collection of matchstick buildings. Grandfather always talked to his matchstick buildings. He talked to them far more than to anyone living; he found their companionship preferable. Irva and I used to visit him often and he always liked to talk to the matchstick buildings far more than he talked to us.

Postmaster Grett, our grandfather, had been constructing matchstick buildings ever since his childhood, when he was plain Master Grett. (How his parents, our great grandparents, would complain when not a single match could be found in the house to light the stove.) Grandfather was a patriotic man – he built replicas only of buildings found in our country. And when off duty he would attend various fairs and competitions for like-minded enthusiasts. He was moderately skilled at his construction with matchsticks and won three medals for his efforts (one for second prize, two for third). He proudly stored these medals in a certain silk-lined drawer, which he would visit often (particularly on unhappy days) and which he would show us too with great ceremony when we were old enough. The saddest day of Grandfather's matchstick career came when the archbishop of Entralla commissioned the ordinary postman Marco Girge (who had won seven medals for first prize) and not Grandfather to build a matchstick model of our cathedral, even though grandfather was the senior postman, even though Grandfather was postmaster. It took Postman Girge, a solitary man who was himself built entirely out of patience, a man who could never do anything with any speed (including his post office rounds), nearly eight years to complete the model. And then, with a ceremony which included the archbishop's blessing, the model was placed on a wooden plinth just by the font, with a collection box at its side.[4] And how

4. SITES OF INTEREST. Entralla Cathedral in miniature. *Postman Girge's matchstick cathedral is still exhibited within our massive stone cathedral to this*

quickly this collection box was filled. How the people loved the matchstick cathedral – more eager, it would seem, to relinquish their money if it might help to keep the matchstick model in good order, than to aid the vast and echoey religious warehouse itself. This is not uncommon; miniature things move people.

Grandfather stopped going to church.

He began to construct his matchstick properties only in private, for himself alone.

Postman Girge was sacked.

As Mother swelled with her pregnancy then, Grandfather back at home undressed himself of his post office blue, approached his drawer of victories in his pants and vest and socks, such was the ritual, and taking out his three medals, carefully pinned them to his vest and, thus attired, having admired himself in his bathroom looking glass, he was finally ready to visit his study. With matchsticks Grandfather built his fragile defences against all the sorrows and difficulties of his life, with a little glue to bind them he was able to construct a kind of contentment. He sat down to make himself a matchstick model of the Central Post Office on Napoleon Street, which was, incidentally, his favourite building to miniaturise – he had made twelve matchstick central post offices already. Though this new model, unlike all the others, lacked any entrance steps.

Mother, standing on bathroom scales watching herself grow, was fascinated, though a little fearful, of her new shape: of what her body factory was producing down there, under the skin. Father, who was invited into the bathroom to note Mother's biological progress through the increasingly large numbers the

---

day, though it is now in ruins, destroyed by a piece of tumbling masonry the size of a man's head; the earthquake broke both the cathedral and the cathedral's model. Today the ruin in matchsticks reminds Entrallans of the ruin in stones, of the broken cathedral before it was fully restored.

arrow indicated, was visibly appalled. When the swelling of her figure was first noticeable he pretended that Mother had been overeating, for it was an unassuming sort of swelling then – a swelling that seemed to mind its own business. But when the protuberance began to take on monstrous proportions, and when its every moment called people's attention to it, and when Mother was forced to adjust the way she walked and sat and moved, then his only desire was to take hold of this immodest extremity and push it back inside Mother until it was out of sight.

Leaving the bathroom Mother and Father entered the largest room of their home – this room was bedroom, kitchen, sitting room, dining room, dressing room, store room. This room was not even a particularly large room, yet the collected possessions of Mother and Father fitted easily enough within it. This room had two windows, one of which looked across Napoleon Street to various police buildings. Their home, a building divided into many small flats, was called Sirkin House. What a tiny little place their fraction of it must have been. Pokey-home. Poxy-home. How inappropriate it is that their love, so huge a thing as it felt to them, could fit within so paltry a container. A thousand, thousand rooms, a palace the size of Versailles in France would have seemed a little more adequate to house the limitlessness of their adoration. But love, how extraordinary this is, does not generally require large quantities of space.

As Mother grew, and as her growth seemed larger than any of the other growths to be found emerging from the pregnant women of our city, Father began to suspect that the removal of the growth would cause Mother some considerable pain. The previous year, Father recalled, he had trapped one of his fingers as he was pulling up some floorboards in the attic of an abandoned building on Foundry Lane, and the finger, once freed, had become unpleasantly large. And to relieve his finger of that largeness, for it looked as if it belonged not to puny father but to some improbable giant, he had pricked it with a needle. And had it hurt? Yes, certainly it had hurt. But then after the pain and after the pus rushed out of him, his finger felt a little better. Sore but better, but only after the pain. And this pain was centred only on a tiny part of himself, on a finger, so how would the pain be if the swelling distorted the whole body? Father looked at sleeping Mother lying on her back, watching the volcano of her belly hidden underneath the sheets, and he began to weep. He crept away from the bed, anxious not to wake Mother, anxious not to disturb the volcano. He shut himself in the bathroom and between heavy sobs rolled and lit himself a soggy cigarette.

So I consider Father now while it's still possible, for regretfully it must be reported that there's little time left for him. There he sits, still enough for examination, on his lavatory seat. As Father smokes his cigarette, there's time to think a little more of this inhaling and exhaling father of ours who was a father-never-to-be.

Father, who were you beyond stamp-licker, post office step-sitter, impregnator?

Our father, Orphan Linas, Linas the Potent, was one of those people who seemed to understand suffering. A child's scream after it has fallen over; an old man hauling in his breath; the everyday bravery a fat woman uses to sit down: the sadness of these things deprived him of sleep.

Sometimes the pain he would see exhibiting itself every day on the city streets would dry up his movement and would stand him rigid, clenched in sorrow. To think that pain was so ordinary, so widespread, that pain was everywhere, that it was impossible to walk out into the streets without witnessing it. How could Father live with this knowledge? I imagine Father now, not atop his lavatory bowl but standing still on a street pavement, the weak engine of his body stalled. His huge eyes are evidence of his sensitivity. His pale skin is so thin you feel you could easily stroke it off. I imagine his eyebrows permanently high on his great forehead, so easily is he surprised, so easily is he distressed. People passing him standing motionless in the street, halted by other people's pain, may think, 'How will his heart last?' Oh,

Father was not a good design, rather he was a failure of nature, a whim perhaps that was not meant to survive long. So large a face, so sad and so timid, but somehow, perhaps because of the honest intensity of its expression, so handsome.

But this night, which I return to now, this night as Father sits on the lavatory seat, he has wept the sorrow out of himself, letting it drip down his face, into his lap, onto his cigarette. With a hiss his cigarette has sighed out of life, and he moves now off his lavatory perch and back into the room where his pregnant wife sleeps on.

So now Father, in search of comfort, turns his mind elsewhere. In his leather satchel, which is locked, even from Mother, is a small part of Father's prodigious collection of foreign stamps. The other stamps, a vast hoard, are secreted away underneath the rotting floorboards of the attic of the abandoned house on Foundry Lane with the dangerous, finger-pinching floorboards. Father collects his satchel and returns to the bathroom and from there he journeys around the world.

With the speed it takes him to place each foreign-stamped envelope in front of the last, he travels from city to city, from continent to continent. He thinks little of crossing from one end of Europe to the other in a second, nor is he impressed, as his fingers pass from envelope to envelope, that he has just strode the enormity of the Atlantic. What does he care for that, he who can traverse the length of long Siberia between breaths, while we lesser beings leave Moscow and take five weeks to arrive in Vladivostok and step onto the railway platform exhausted and angry. Watch him sniff and kiss those stamps. His fingers, his eyes, his lips do all the travelling. This childish man, who is our father, is attempting to breathe in, to see, to feel all the smells, sights and touches of the world in one greedy instant.

Father, who would never travel beyond our country's borders, was fascinated by the world. So what, thought Father, if the stamps had been franked, if their innocence had been deprived them, so what when they had come from a foreign country, when it was a foreign person, whose life Father struggled to comprehend, who performed the franking. And he often wondered: what is the taste of foreign stamp glue?

Father had stolen every stamp in his foreign stamp collection. He stole them from work, from the post office. He stole the international post. If an envelope came to our city with 'AIR MAIL' or 'PAR AVION' proudly written on it, it may just as well have said 'MAIL FOR LINAS'.

True, Father was really only interested in the stamps – he paid little attention to the envelopes. But how could he deliver letters with the stamps missing – what would people say to that? What excuse could he possibly give? No, he could not risk delivery, so he kept the letters to himself. Though he loved only the stamps, he kept the envelopes as well. At first he believed he would deliver all the foreign letters in time, that he was just holding onto them for as long as his love of the stamps lasted. But his love for the stamps would not be sated, it would not be tamed.

Sometimes of course there would be complaints that certain letters had not arrived, but such losses could be easily explained: it was due, of course, with apologies, to the lamentable state of the mail service. The missing letters were placed on a list in Grandfather's office. Letters have a habit of getting lost, it's just one of the hazards of sending mail. International mail is particularly problematic. At first nobody noticed that the complaints concerning missing letters all came from the district of the city where only Father delivered the mail. Until one particular letter failed to arrive.

It didn't really matter that Mirgarita Gavala's letter from her son in Valencia, Spain (with a light-blue stamp – labelled España – of King Juan Carlos II at a value of eight pesetas), didn't arrive – she didn't suppose that the boy would be so considerate as to write to his ailing mother anyway. It didn't really matter that the response to a sheaf of poems the poet Angel Berg had sent off to a publishing house in London, England (with a ten-and-a-half pence stamp of the Abbey and Palace of Holyroodhouse, and with the outline of the head of Queen Elizabeth II in the top right-hand corner), never turned up because the letter was a rejection anyway. But it was a shame that the cog sent in a little brown cardboard box all the way from Zurich, Switzerland (with two stamps, both labelled Helvetica: the first, the most colourful, for two francs, celebrating 800 Jahre of the Stadt Luzern; the second for seven francs, saying Championnat du monde de Dressage Lausanne), which would have been able to fix the ancestral and beautiful antique clock of Marian Stashak in time for his father Maurice's eightieth birthday, never appeared. In any case there was little trauma caused by all these failed intentions that had embarked so optimistically (or not) from all those distant buildings, those distant hands and lands. Since their arrival may not have been expected, their absence often caused no tears, and people continued their quiet or noisy days unaware of the information that had been stolen from them for the sake of various colourful or monochrome rectangles of paper. But then someone in one of the smaller of the governmental offices missed a letter that he was certain should have arrived and reported the absence with a swiftness that betrayed how new he was to his position.

Ambras Cetts, for such was the young man's name, will go far, and the more we want him to fail (for his eagerness has deeply offended) the higher he will rise.[5]

The letter Ambras Cetts registered as missing did not even contain any particularly important information. To be precise it boasted the official results of a recreational pistol match held at a shooting gallery in Vienna, Austria, between various civil servants from various civic authorities who were assembled in that city

---

5. ENTRALLANS OF NOTE. Ambras Jonas Cetts. Former Mayor. *Perhaps some people may feel, considering this man with his dazzling future, perfect features and healthy body, that he is the hero this history has so far failed to produce. And in a way, a kind of way, he is.*

for seminars on the rise of vermin internationally, specifically on that menace *Rattus rattus*. (The stamp was for four schillings and was pink and labelled Republik Österreich and was of someone called Almsee.) Our country on that occasion was represented by a certain A. J. Cetts who would not have been interested in this missing piece of trivia had it not been for the fact that he had won the competition and was eager to present the proof to his superior at the earliest possible opportunity. When the score sheet failed to arrive, Cetts called up the shooting gallery and was informed that the sheet had already been posted to him some week and a half ago. It had certainly been lost. Another score sheet was sent (this time with a six-schilling stamp of Lindauer Hütte Rätikon, also labelled Republik Österreich), but when that failed to arrive, after another week and a half, Ambras Cetts decided to take matters into his own hands. He marched to the Central Post Office with two of his colleagues, all uniformed in perfectly fitting suits.

Only one post office employee was absent from the post office as Ambras Cetts and his colleagues began their investigation, and that was Mother, whose waters had broken early that morning. Soon our faint beats would be joining with all the other hearts' soft drumming throughout the world, soon the world would be bursting into technicolour.

Father was seated that morning on his stool by Mother's empty plastic chair, as tense as an overwound spring. Unable to bear the pain coming out of Mother's great mouth, he had rushed from the hospital into the comfort of the post office the moment she had started screaming.

As Mother wailed for God and for Father, and expressed an eagerness for her life to be ended, Ambras Cetts discovered on our postmaster grandfather's desk a list of letters reported missing, which all happened to have originated from foreign countries. As the list was further examined – as we lessened Mother's struggles for a kind (and brief) moment – the streets of the complainants were considered, and a map of the city was sought . . . and found on the wall behind Grandfather's desk.[6]

This map, a generous size, probably the most comprehensive map of Entralla at that time, was not, however, in the pristine state it had been purchased in. Years of post office dust and labour; years of the exhalations of the post office workers' nicotine-tainted breaths had bent its corners upwards and made brittle its surface. Generations of employees had been called into the postmaster's office to offer their many thousands of excuses, both the believable and the fantastic, to list over time all the illnesses that are available to the human body in this part of the world and to elaborate on the processes of these illnesses; or to tell tales of innocent and guilty colleagues; or to express predictable Christmas sentiments; or to be dismissed without a smile; or to shake hands on retirement day and then to look finally at that large map behind Grandfather's desk for the ultimate time, briefly to view the network of streets, the honeycomb of our lives, before retreating in old age to a life that concerned only a handful of passageways.

This map had been disfigured by something other than time and the deposits of so many human fingers. It had lines drawn over it in standard black biro, dividing the city into even more sections than already existed. These boundaries were not real walls of bricks, they were not present in our everyday sleeping and waking city; they were the barriers demarcating the streets and districts assigned to the postmen. Each division belonged to one man. And each division had been impaled with a pin on which a piece of fixed paper stuck out at right angles, like a diminutive flag. Each of these toy flags, as if they were to indicate principalities of a country, had a surname written in capitals across it: the name not of the local potentate but of the postman

6. INCIDENTALLY – *For the following paragraphs it may be useful to view the map at the front of this book.*

who delivered the letters for that portion of the city. Oh what a useful map this is, thought Ambras Cetts and his colleagues. Three minutes was all it took these achievers to discover the patch on the city's surface in which all the letters had failed to arrive. A single postman's division.

L. Dapps said the flag. Where is this Dapps?, wondered Ambras Cetts and his companions. We'll speak to this Dapps before the minute is out. To ask him what? To ask him: how is it possible that all these letters should disappear from one district only? One district for which only one postman delivers the letters? One postman who handled not one but all of the absent articles? Is that coincidental or is that criminal? Which one of those, answer us that.

Now I imagine that I can hear a noise. A sharp noise to provoke ear covering. The sound of the postal horn perhaps? No, no, it is the scream of a woman in labour as she pushes, pants and sweats. This is agony. Mother's between-the-legs door, our door into the world, is beginning to open, it's ripping open. But wait a minute – as Mother screams, the door of the postmaster's office is opened from within. This door should be screaming just like Mother, but, as if mocking my dramatic intentions, it scarcely makes a sound. As Mother continues to scream, something begins to come out of her, something breathing and bloody. At exactly the instant that this life starts to emerge, the door to Grandfather's office is opened with a barely audible murmur, and three men in suits come out into the post office's dusty hall.

'Dapps. Which one is Dapps?' What a question! Surely no one will answer it. But Marta Stroud of counter three unfortunately insists on informing them of her existence by placing her hand up in the air.

Marta Stroud's ugly, hairy arm is in the air, still wobbling from the action that put it there, and shan't, can't, won't be ignored. Marta Stroud who is made more eager by her psoriasis, as if her over-helpfulness might compensate for her unpleasant disfigurement. Marta Stroud with the blotches on her that are islands of mould, as though her disease had stretched a globe across her face – but it is not our globe, it is not the Earth exhibited on her skin; none of the countries are recognisable. Her arm, equally distorted with clumps of islands, bogland most likely, is still spread upwards and her body, the many continents of discoloured itchiness concealed beneath her touch-me-not clothing, joins it now, standing erect on the points of its suffering toes, as if Marta Stroud and her whole map of mould are sure to touch beyond countless universes in their attempt to attract attention. It is this same Marta Stroud who has finally now been noticed, this same Marta Stroud who has formed her body into a pointing device, yes, it is this Mould, this Moist, this Marta Stroud, who is volunteering, when no volunteers were asked for, the information that Father, our father, visibly frightened now, sitting on his wooden stool by Mother's plastic seat at the twelfth counter, holding his heart while his mouth urgently searches for air, that Father, our father – I'm nearing the end now, Father's time is nearly up – that this man is the one they are asking for. He is, in fact, simply, unquestionably, guiltfully . . . Dapps!

In a ward in the maternity hospital on Saint Mirgarita of Antioch Street (patron saint of pregnant women, who died in the Roman city of Antioch, now the Turkish city of Antakya), Dallia Dapps gave birth to two little girls. She named them Alva and Irva.

Our birth certificate revealed that Linas Dapps was our father, though it did not reveal that Father was not present at the birth of us, his two daughters, or that when Dallia Lizbet Dapps, née Grett, screamed at the pain of giving birth to her two girls, she should perhaps also have been screaming out for the life of her husband.

Alva Lina Dapps and Irva Lina Dapps. Identical twins with identical wails. I came first. Irva waited two more hours and then was forced to decide, after some exhausting coercion from Mother, that it was safe to come out. She never really wanted to come out, she'd rather have stayed in there all the while, she never really wanted to come out at all.

Interlude 1
Coffee

Market Square

Market Square is found easily enough on Arsenal Street in easy walking distance from Cathedral Square, and is always a worthwhile place to visit. The square abounds in cafés: there are no less than twelve open every weekday; on weekends five are available to accommodate the Saturday evening adolescents in search of noise and love and beer; or three are open for the benefit of the

Café Louis

Sunday morning stroller in search of coffee and peace, but who may become irritated by the sudden arrival of the after-church family crowd. On Wednesdays, market day, the square is of course particularly busy and populated by many stalls selling fresh produce, electronic equipment, a wide variety of second-hand clothes, religious amulets, antiques, plastic objets d'art. The buildings that surround the square are all fifteenth century with terracotta tiles and wooden beams. But sadly, due to our earth-quake, many are replicas.

CAFÉ LOUIS
Market Square 14   Open 10:00–23:30   Tel. 316 80 24

Café Louis, a red building with 'LOUIS' clearly marked on its front (in any case the café with the wonky awning, is where I would recommend our distinguished foreign visitors take their morning coffee break. If on entering you are initially disgusted by the smell of tobacco smoke, do not immediately rush out in search of another café – all cafés have this smell: we are a nation of smokers. Instead, allow the smell to remind you of Linas; it is good that you should consider Linas now.

I have suggested this café not solely because it is one of those places which offers a 10 per cent reduction to all readers of this book. (Though this should of course be taken advantage of – and be sure to exhibit the book each time the waitress comes forward, and perhaps even to point at it indiscreetly.) But I recommend the café also for its excellent thick, bowel-moving coffee. In fact not even purely for the coffee, or the 10 per cent reduction, has this place been selected above all others; nor is it even for the scores of beautiful late-teenage waitresses that Louis has employed over the decades of his café's existence to soften the hearts of hard old men and make them linger and care less for the thickness of their wallets. No, the principal reason for my recommendation is that sitting amongst you now as you drink the faultless coffee are *various men and women from our city, regulars at Café Louis, who happen also to be characters (or the children of characters) from this book.*

Let us start with the couple in the darkest corner of the bar, two men, both sitting with coffee or beer in front of them, not talking but with anxious expressions on their faces, as if they dare not talk, as if they are waiting for something or someone. One is older, he is tall and podgy and nervous, he drums his fingers on the table's surface; the other, shorter with greying hair, sighs noisily every now and then. But these two characters have yet to be introduced in this history (perhaps that is why they are so impatient), so let us leave them alone for the time being with their secret anticipation. Let us turn instead to Louis himself, for he is invariably there, or at least his body is – his mind travels increasingly longer distances until one day, surely not far from now, it will never come back. Look at stationary Louis: what a wonderful wrinkled old fellow he is. Look how white his hair is, see how mildly he looks ahead – he had such a temper once that he smashed all the dozens of coffee cups and all the lines of beer glasses one evening, two decades back (out of love), as if all those glasses and cups were the containers of his happiness, and so had to be broken because he was miserable. Louis, even in his more active days, will never perform a major role in this history, though when his hair was black, his café was frequently visited by Alva Dapps, who liked to rest here from her walks around Entralla.

Please note the wooden seat next to Louis. It is empty. It is always empty now. It was once filled with the ample behind of a man named Kurt Laudus. Here rests, if not a character from this book, then a ghost of a character from this book. The Kurt who once sat on this stool was the same Kurt who once worked in our Central Post Office, but who was never, despite a postmaster's hopes, to fall in love with one Dallia Dapps, née Grett. Kurt loved only men, and his greatest love was Louis, a love which Louis's customers never spoke openly about, for such a love was officially prohibited then. Kurt once squandered Louis's ever-

constant attentions on a student of archaeology from Entralla University, and it was because of this that Louis smashed all his cups and glasses and also, a short while later, Kurt's face.

But Kurt Laudus has left us now, embraced by a collapsing building one July 16th, during our earthquake adventure. The chair is occupied only by memory: histories from the brain of a vague and snow-white, gently dying, mourning lover.

Here also should be, slouched over the bar, nonchalantly working through one of the day's many tall, half-pint glasses of local blonde beer (highly recommended, incidentally), Lavinja Cetts, Ambras Cetts's daughter. You will remember at what promise-filled moment we left Ambras's career (and what results his over-eagerness had on the progression of the twins' history). Well, here now is his forty-year-old daughter, shaking slightly, aggressive with loneliness and stooped over by it also, who is paying the price for the phenomenally successful life of her impeccable father.

Enjoy your coffee.

Part Two

ALVA & IRVA

An Over-Protective Mother
Once Lived on Veber Street

Residential Streets

Taking trolley bus 5 – heading out of the city, away from Cathedral and Market Squares – you will quickly find yourself entering a residential area of the city. Do not be frightened. Here is where the real stories are kept, not in the larger, more imposing structures of Entralla's centre, but rather inside its ordinary domestic dwellings. Certainly the guidebook to our city will not advise you to take

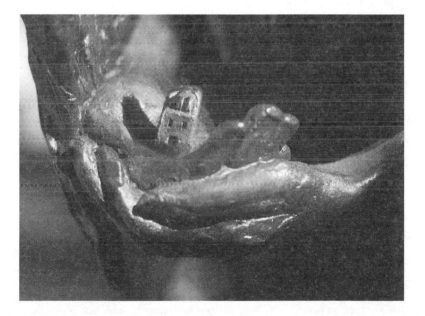

27 Veber Street

trolley bus route 5, unless it is heading in the opposite direction, but that is one of many failings of that book. Take the stop at Pilias Street in sector eight of our city, from there it is a short stroll to Veber Street, where this chapter shall be focused.

★ ★ ★

Mother held at each breast an Alva or an Irva. While I struggled and wriggled with life, unable to lose the feeling of delight for movement, Irva kept very still. Only her eyes seemed to move, following Mother's actions with the disapproving look of an ancient. I was easy to feed, clamping my mouth to Mother's nipples and sucking with so ferocious an energy that Mother believed she could feel herself emptying out. But Irva had to be carefully encouraged; she kept turning her heavy head away from the nipples as if away from life, and often Mother had to feed her with a bottle, and often she was sick.

This is how we looked, these were the gifts we were given: from Mother pale skin and dark hair; from Father big heads and weak hearts. Not much of an inheritance.

Mother returned to her flat on Napoleon Street with two more little lives than she had left it and with one less big one. How the flat smelt of Father. From one window she could look out and see Napoleon Street down which Father had been escorted away from the post office towards the police buildings, already so pale, already with strange shooting pains in his arm. Whenever she looked out of the window, Mother saw Father being taken away again and again. In her mind she saw him, night and day, being escorted down the street, and, once out of sight, quickly reappearing again, still under escort, still crying the same tears. And no one ever came running to help him. Weak and dreamy Orphan Linas, Linas the Potent, our tall father, had miserably confessed to Ambras Cetts and his companions everything about letters from foreign countries and everything about an abandoned house on Foundry Lane with dangerous floorboards. What he had done was criminal, they told him. What he had done would not go unpunished. What he had done meant that he would have to accompany them immediately on an excursion to the police station. And suddenly Father knew that he would never see Mother again, because here he was, flanked by men on either side, being walked out of the post office and up Napoleon Street, surely (of this he felt certain) on the way to his execution. He stood swaying in the police station, even though there was no breeze. The floor started rushing towards him. And everything went dark.

'Linas Dapps: extinct of a weak heart', the report states. He simply slumped forwards. A doctor's note stapled to the report mentioned the words 'Systole', 'Ventricle' and 'Atrium' and concluded with the words 'Mitral Insufficiency'.

Mother realised that if she were to care properly for us, if she were to keep our baby hearts twitching, then she must find some place where the window offered a different view. So Mother left her home, where she had played briefly the role of wife, and entered a new one where she would perform as Mother. And for that she permitted Grandfather to help. Grandfather rented a house on Veber Street, in sector eight of Entralla, far away from post offices, opera houses, theatres and police rooms.

There was a time when we knew everyone in Veber Street. There were the Misons, mother, father, son, daughter, who had their toy shop on Pilias Street, who all had red hair, except for the daughter who was blonde. There was Plint the butcher, his meagre wife and their aggressive daughter. There was Miss Stott the tailor who seemed ancient when I first remember her but who continued to be ancient, her ancientness becoming ever more convincing over the following years. There was Fiff the baker who lived with his red-faced wife, whom he was rumoured to have beaten frequently, and their three sons over at number twenty three. And there was Jonas Lutt who lived on his own, but who was very rarely at home, and who had just become a long-distance lorry driver.

For a while Veber Street and those streets that connected to it were all that we needed to know of the world, it was our corner of existence, our village in a city, Entralla in microcosm. Everything that we learnt and saw could be contained within it: Veber Street, Pilias Street, Umper Street, Hill Street, W. Glinsky Street and Eemar Walk. Pilias Street was our Mecca, since it contained the most shops (we supposed then that there was nowhere else so colourful, nowhere so populated), and beyond it lay places and people we scarcely even thought of. But mainly, and certainly to begin with, it was just Veber Street for us.

We do not recall our arrival on Veber Street, we were too young. But surely one day we did arrive and once inside our new home Mother shut the door behind her and closed all the shutters on the ground floor. When the people of the street came knocking in the hope of introducing themselves, Mother would not answer. When Mother shopped for her provisions she left us at home, safe, she presumed, huddled up together, surrounded by the bars of our shared cot. And as she shopped she would not allow herself to be drawn into conversation.

Our poor mother had become a mother and a widow on the same day at the age of seventeen. Mother's brain had formed the words 'recluse', 'hermit', 'anchorite' and 'misanthrope', and found it liked them very much. Mother had decided never to let anyone come into her home, no. 27 Veber Street, except for the inevitable prying glare from her visiting father. There would be no such thing even as Veber Street for us baby girls, the world would be reduced to no. 27. But '27' was what was written on the outside of the house, and so that too must be lost. All that was important were the rooms and levels of this new home. In this new world the continents of Africa and America and Asia would not be permitted to exist, nor would the great blueness of the Pacific and Indian and Atlantic oceans. The world had become dehydrated, it had withered and shrunk and breathed in until it had taken on the exact dimensions of a house in our city.

The first thing, Irva used to tell me, that she could ever remember was waking up alone. She sensed that she was about to die. She screamed and screamed. Mother came in and put on the lights, and there was I on the floor. Limp Alva. I'd banged my head. I'd managed to climb over the bars of the cot and got out. Mother fixed the bars higher.

These were our first words.
  Irva: 'Alva'.
  Alva: 'Alva'.

Sometimes we would play under the kitchen table with wooden building blocks and also with Lego from the country of Denmark. I did the building, Irva passed the bricks to me. And sometimes Mother would read to us.

Mother had one book with her for company, a manual on baby care (translated from the English), which she read and reread as if its ordered chapters and recommendations were some profound treatise or the collected works of a master poet. In much the same way as people recite great memorised chunks of the Bible in moments of distress, in later life Mother would incongruously quote from her book on babies. I remember her, years after Irva and I had grown up, whispering this one day in the kitchen as she was waiting for the kettle to boil: 'To burp the child place him in an upright position against your shoulder and gently pat his back or behind to help him bring up his wind. Do not be frustrated when baby refuses to burp, it does not mean that he is ill or abnormal; sometimes this process takes time. When he burps, consider that a victory. And congratulate yourself.'

Over the years Mother's freckles, the one remnant of her

childhood, faded. Her stomach grew to keep her depression company. Her depression was there to keep alive the memory of Father. She fed it well, she stroked it, she looked after it. It was her miserable, heavy friend. The memory of Father was evident to us throughout our childhood in the form of a wooden, three-legged stool. Mother had Grandfather bring Father's stool from the post office to our home in Veber Street. The stool always stood on a side table in the kitchen, where we were frequently encouraged to consider it, to touch it even; to begin with Irva and I believed our mysterious father was a stool and not a person at all. On special occasions Mother would take the stool down from its table and allow us to sit on it. We'd take it in turns to sit on the stool. When I was sitting on the stool, Irva would sit on my lap and vice versa. And, a little later, but I'll mention it now since we're considering Father and his stool, Grandfather said, looking at the stool, 'Some people, like some buildings, are built well and last long; others, poorly constructed, soon collapse. It's how it is. Rootless. No foundations. What did you expect?'

The early death of Father had made Mother morbid. She was horrified at how complicated human beings are; she didn't understand all those components and wires within every one of us; she feared that once something had gone wrong inside, no matter how slight, death must inevitably follow. She was terrified of illnesses, at how many there were out there in the world, beyond our home, at how they waited for their moment in and around other humans. She saw death all over the city, all over the streets. Every sneezing passer-by meant to pass chronic pneumonia onto us; every shop owner sprinkled arsenic on his products; every car and every trolley bus harboured desires to swerve up onto the pavement. Whenever she looked at us she could see us dead. She saw our slumped forms in horrible poses, after a multitude of expirations. Asphyxiated by leaking gas. Drowned in the bath. With our skulls shattered after we had fallen from a window. She could never relax her protection, never once; the moment she did, Irva or I, or perhaps both of us, would cease to be. Of this she was certain. Each morning when she found us alive, she took hold of her book on baby care, kissed its cover and blessed it.

There was little then to differentiate us from each other. Our eyes were the same shade of blue, our hair the same length and colour, our skin was identically pale and thin and revealed the same streams of blue-green veins on our big foreheads and on our arms and legs. But sometimes Mother would see me pressing myself against the front door, peering cautiously through the keyhole. And at other times she might open the large cupboard in the kitchen where the saucepans were kept to find Irva inside, huddled up in the darkness.

It was of course Grandfather and not Mother who took us on our first remembered excursions out into the world. First in a pushchair, a double pushchair with twin seats, and later, taking each of us by a hand, he would take us out to see Veber Street and sometimes even some of what existed beyond (but never past Pilias Street). And people, women mostly, would often stop Grandfather, and together they would talk about us, and sometimes our heads would be patted (which we never liked), and often, from our pushchair or later standing either side of, and probably even clinging to, Grandfather's legs, we would hear the word, 'Lovely', or the sentence 'Aren't they gorgeous?' But always, always, 'How can you tell them one from the other, postmaster?' And of course he would have to reply, 'Well, actually I can't, but their mother can.' And the other person would respond with the air of an expert, 'Well, yes, you'd expect that, wouldn't you, that's the maternal bond, isn't it?'

Among the many gifts Grandfather bought us was a stamp album. How overjoyed he was while watching us peer through our (identical) magnifying glasses, examining so studiously all the little colourful squares of paper. But Grandfather was never once permitted to bring us foreign stamps. Mother was quite clear about that. And just to make sure, all the stamps were examined by her before being passed on (with what nostalgia did she one day inspect a set of stamps depicting beetles), for death was lurking in those foreign stamps. Our weak and dreamy father had been taken in by their bright and beautiful colours; it wouldn't happen to us.

And so came the time of our first adventures in plasticine. Grandfather was the one who supplied us with our first packet of plasticine: multicoloured strips, clean and corrugated, neatly covered in transparent sheets of plastic to prevent them from becoming dirty and sheathed in a bright red cardboard box. The front of the box bore the legend 'HERKIN'S PLASTICINE', the reverse 'HERKIN'S TOYS, 12–23 MIRCAN STREET, SECTOR 2, ENTRALLA 2006'. Grandfather had shown us some of his matchstick children, but had urged us not to come too close, never to touch. We had sat watching him, sitting holding hands on the sofa, rigid with attention, such informative hours contemplating Grandfather carefully building away. But when it had come to our turn to build with matchsticks, when grandfather had reluctantly sacrificed a few matchsticks and a blob of glue, our creations had been a great disappointment. We were unable to make matchsticks resemble anything other than . . . matchsticks. So Grandfather bought us plasticine, an easier building material. Suitable for novices; ages four and up.

At first we made nothing more miraculous than multicoloured spheres comprised of all the different strips of plasticine moulded into one marbled, curdling riot of colour. These spheres collected dust and dirt and frustrated us enormously because, once mixed, the colours were almost impossible to separate. In time, with greater patience we made other things: birds so ill-proportioned that they could never fly, mongrel dogs of indiscernible parentage, houses that would never stand up for long. But that was all it took; we had worked out how malleable plasticine was. We had worked out that, with care, structures that remained standing could perhaps be erected; from plasticine we could fashion the world in miniature.

We spent much time in the attic looking out of the window (despite Mother's protestations) onto Veber Street, wondering about all the life there. And one day I decided, and Irva cautiously agreed, to make a model of the street, not just a quick model that would take us a few hours to build, but a complex work that would take weeks and perhaps even months to finish: a highly detailed miniaturisation of exactly what was seen from our window. It was constructed entirely from red blocks of plasticine which we purchased with Grandfather from the Misons' toy shop. How difficult it was to learn the buildings of Veber Street. How we struggled to see them properly for the first time. How plasticine helped us to understand.

But our first real plasticine model was unskilled and inaccurate. We lacked the patience at this early stage, and it was abandoned after only five days' work. But it was historically, crucially, inevitably from those days onwards that our fingers always smelled of plasticine.

Then came Grandfather's unpleasant and aggressive visits. He demanded we spend our days out in Veber Street, where other children played. Grandfather said we mustn't spend all day indoors, he even shouted at Mother. He thought that it would have been better if he had never shown us his matchstick masterpieces; that he would have done better to have brought us up on a diet of stamps. Stamps every day. And now what had happened to those stamps he had given us? They remained neglected in our bedroom; he hadn't seen us studying them for months. Would we ever grow up to be worthy of the post office, which he hoped would one day be father to us fatherless girls? Now, whenever Grandfather came to visit, he would begin by hauling us down from our attic hideout and pushing us, despite Mother's hysterical fear and protestations, into Veber Street, bellowing at us all the while. He would not be placated, even when Mother desperately rattled a box of kitchen matches in his face.

On Grandfather's first unpleasant visit (after he had yelled at us – 'Go on then, go and make friends!'), we two, sitting on our front doorstep, with the front door locked behind us, came to an important decision: that Mother had been lying. Because if Mother wasn't lying we would be dead.

'If you're out of my sight or out of your grandfather's sight, even for a moment, you'll die.' That's what Mother said. It had happened once before, she told us. On the only day that Mother had been unable to be with Father, on the day we were born, Father had suddenly collapsed. And all because Mother couldn't see him. That's what Mother said. And so, as we sat on the doorstep together, where neither Mother nor Grandfather could see us, we had to conclude that Mother had been lying. But, we asked each other that day, what would happen if we were to lose sight of each other? We shuddered at the horror. What would happen if we were to be separated, properly separated: yes, what then? This evil was considered by us for many minutes on the doorstep, and we concluded that separation, true separation, would surely be the death of us. It was because of our hearts of course, we decided, which had magnets in them, or cogs, or switches or some such, that worked only if they were close together. Each, we decided together on the doorstep, sent out signals to the other, complicated signals. And those signals, those codes, kept our hearts beating. 'If we were to be truly separated,' I said to Irva, 'then there would be no more Irva.' 'Nor,' said Irva to me, 'would there be any more Alva.'

Sometimes we would spend the afternoons with Miss Stott the tailor, who would call us over as we sat all melancholic on the doorstep to our home like novel versions of the stone lions that sometimes adorn the driveways of country estates. From us Miss Stott relearnt her love for the rolls of material on her shelves. We used to stroke them and smell them, sitting for hours with patches of fabric on our laps, our fingers tracing out the many patterns. Our enthusiasm reminded Miss Stott of the period of her amorous adventure with a man named Gebbs, and of a time when they both lived in the Tailoring District in sector five, and of how Gebbs, who was also a tailor, had promised that he would one day marry (though he never actually specified whom he would marry – but then Miss Stott never thought there was any need to specify). She remembered Gebbs had told her how he was able to make an ugly man beautiful, just by providing him with the right suit. He told her how he chose the correct patterns for his clients and transformed them, because of the excellence of their new suits, from shy, awkward beings into successful businessmen. But once Gebbs realised that Miss Stott's belly was stretching her dresses and that a new tailor was even then beginning to imagine new patterns and suits inside the belly of Miss Stott, he hurriedly abandoned her. Miss Stott, when she discovered that Gebbs was to marry one of the daughters of a distinguished tailor on Saclinn Street, had broken into Gebbs's shop in the middle of the night and with a pair of sharp tailoring scissors had carefully cut all his suits in half. She left a note for Gebbs, saying: 'These suits are called broken promises suits, or half-truths suits.'

Soon afterwards Miss Stott moved to our district and set up her own tailor's shop and kept her son in a playpen behind the counter, until, after a while, he grew up and grew away from her, he grew up and grew away to such an extent that he went off to live in another city altogether, a city so distant from Entralla that he saw his mother only twice every year. From Miss Stott we learnt the great new words 'warp', 'weft', 'worsted', 'polyester', 'multiple plain weave', 'lightweight cotton' and also the precious word 'corduroy', which was the name of a material originally worn by the kings of France. How that one word suggested a world and a time so far away. 'Corduroy' I would often whisper to myself as if it were a secret, 'corduroy, corduroy'. Sometimes we dressed each other up in old dead people's suits which Miss

Stott kept at the back of her shop, reserved for the poorest of her customers. Or Miss Stott would arrange our black hair in the styles of her youth, and sometimes she would let us wear some of her old dresses (or occasionally two new ones), and we would dance to old records made by old dead people, and how we felt alive then. At the end of our joyful afternoons, the pair of us, wearing nothing but voluminous dress shirts, would calm ourselves down in Miss Stott's sitting room, sipping the orangeade she bought for us. Miss Stott would tell us the complete history of Veber Street, from when it was part of the countryside many, many years ago, right up to the latest news of the week. She was the self-appointed historian of our street. She knew all its characters, all its crimes and sorrows. She told us of the family who used to live in our house and had all gone to live in Melbourne, Australia; she told us that the Plints used to have a son as well as a daughter, but that the son had died in a car accident; she told us that Mr Fiff, the baker, beat his wife; she told us that she'd seen Mr Plint, the butcher, and Mrs Misons, the toy shop owner's wife, in one of the side streets kissing with tongues, with Mr Plint's hands on Mrs Misons' breasts, and that, she supposed, might be the reason that Mrs Misons' youngest child had blonde hair like Mr Plint rather than the ginger it ought to have, like Mr Misons. She was a very knowledgeable woman. She'd often sit on the doorstep of the tailor's shop just watching the street, gathering its little histories. Some people, we would notice over the years, would yell at Miss Stott as she sat there – 'Stop staring at us! Quit your nosing!' But Miss Stott would go on staring, always fascinated. In those days we wanted nothing more than to listen to the commonplace histories of Veber Street.

But all this time Mother was not happy; she was jealous of the old woman. When we returned home with gifts of old dresses and trinkets from the indulgent Miss Stott, she would hide the trinkets and bleach the dresses. And Grandfather was unhappy too. When he had demanded we make friends, he had meant friends with our contemporaries, he was not happy to have us spend the rest of our days in the company of an introspective old crone (as he described our friend). Soon afterwards came the time when we were walked out from Vebcr Street every day, always in the company of Grandfather, beyond even Pilias Street, beyond the limits of our imagination, into previously undiscovered possibilities of existence. On that first day of our discovery of new territory, Irva, terrified, vomited on the pavement. But even so, Grandfather insisted we carried on going despite the sick and despite the tears I was shedding for Irva. We walked, on those outings, to a street called Littsen Street. There was a long wall on Littsen Street in the centre of which were some unpleasant-looking cast-iron gates. On those outings we always walked up to the gates, never beyond the gates, never through the gates. Only up to them, and then back home: preparation for a horror yet to come.

And then one day, incredibly, surprisingly, Grandfather ordered us to go and visit our friend Miss Stott. We did not understand then the deception behind Grandfather's command. Miss Stott had made each of us a set of clothes, each identical to the other, but we thought nothing of this, we had always worn identical clothing. But we did notice that this set was smarter than the other sets, and had a blazer with it.

Other people wanted us now, and Mother would have to let those other people have us promptly at nine every morning. Mercifully though they would allow her to retrieve us at four o'clock every afternoon. If we did not change hands every day at those hours, which was, incidentally, the law, we would be taken away from Mother permanently 'It's all for the good,' Grandfather told Mother, 'the law is correct. This law is the best thing that could happen to them. It may be a little hard to begin with, but they cannot stay at home all their lives.'

So every day, in sombre preparation, as the date came ever closer, we walked up to the gates with Grandfather, nervously, with terror on our faces. And then one morning Mother scrunched up her pudgy hands into little fists, rubbed her leaking eyes and bade goodbye to her twin loves, who arrived on Littsen

Street to find the gates were open and to see that there were noisy and rough children everywhere. On that day a woman we had never seen before came up to Grandfather and said, 'Alva and Irva Dapps?' And Grandfather nodded, and the woman said, 'Thank you, you may leave them now, goodbye Postmaster.' And Grandfather, looking somewhat anxious, on this terrible day when we learnt that even his great authority had limits, left Irva and me all alone with this woman we had never seen before.

A Set of Female Twins Once
Attended the School on Littsen Street

The Littsen Street Educational Establishment

Nos. 75–125 Littsen Street made up the collection of buildings that were designed specifically to contain the difficult business of educating children. The buildings had a high wall around them to keep knowledge in and ignorance out, and, in the mid point of the wall that gave onto the street, a formidable iron gate. The architect of this school either received a pitifully small budget in which to

The Pulvin Street School

complete his brief, or else he lacked any imagination, or else he was one of those undeniably cunning individuals who realise that no matter how sincere a child's intention to study may be, that child is, on occasion, liable to look out of the classroom window in the hope of distraction. Thus he ensured that the architecture on view from any of the school buildings onto any other of the school buildings contained very few distractional properties. Unfortunately, blocks of domestic dwellings today stand in the school's place. However, the school on Pulvin Street (a short walk from the University or Market Square, see map), which was constructed at the same time, though at the other end of the city, is identical, and a visit there will give much the same impression.

★ ★ ★

In the playground the teacher instructed us all to follow her into our form, into that room which would become so familiar. When we saw the desks we felt a little relieved. 'Two people to a desk!' we whispered to each other, 'Alva and Irva: desk-mates!' And then the teacher began to instruct each child where to sit. Just after she had called out Alva Dapps, the first shock came. The name of the person to be sitting next to me was not Irva Dapps, but a small girl with long brown hair impeccably plaited, who was called Eda Dapps.

But to be separated! And so soon! The pain stopped us from thinking, stopped us from moving, and stopped all of us from working, except for our eyes, which immediately summoned tears. There we stood in front of the classroom with all the other children around us (except for those with names that came before ours alphabetically and except for Eda – whose name had come between us – who had obediently taken her place): lachrymose pillars, rigid in our disobedience, holding hands which we were determined would never come unfastened. The teacher asked which of us was called Alva, but neither of us responded. She smiled then, asked us again in a kind voice, but we wouldn't look at her face, nor answer her. When she asked us once more, the voice was still kind, but we could detect a note of harshness underneath it. There was nastiness in this woman; she smelt of pencil shavings, and that was not an encouraging smell, speaking as it did of sharp points. She asked us again which was Alva, and to add to the possibilities, as if the situation was not confusing and distressing enough, which was Irva. But really we were both Alva and we were both Irva then. We remained jaw-locked in our misery and rather than looking at her face we regarded her hair, which was tied up into the tightest little bun on the top of her head, like a mean version of a halo on a statue of an almost-saint. But our considerations of Miss Aynk – for such was that piece of authority's name (and it was a name that would never leave her, but would stick to her like a tattoo, refusing her marriage) – were interrupted by her bony hands which leapt forwards now and took hold of the wrists of those hands of ours which were joined.

She actually touched us! The horror of a teacher touching a pupil. They should learn to keep their distance. Just as there are signs 'Keep Off the Grass', there should be signs 'Do Not Touch the Pupils'. And there was such strictness, such firmness, such domination in that unwelcome touch. And such cold hands too, hands that had never been warmed by love. Hands that had spent far too long sharpening pencils. And then, she severed us!

And we began to shake, our whole formerly twinned but now bisected bodies grimly twitched, a dance to this cruelty, and the tears flooded out now, and everything was shifting out of focus. We were going to die, this was it, we were going to die. And we waited for the darkness to come. But then, oh bless her beautiful plaits, Eda stood up and said, 'Please, Miss Aynk, I think they want to sit together.' 'Do you?' Miss Aynk asked. And then we found we could nod. Aynk said, 'I am a tolerant woman. Would Eda Dapps mind sitting next to Stepan Dinkin?' 'No, miss.' But would Stepan Dinkin mind sitting next to Eda Dapps? And then Stepan Dinkin emerged from the mass behind us to expose himself as a healthy-looking boy with curly mousy hair and even, how extraordinary this was, with his left ear pierced, and this ear-pierced seven-year-old responded negatively to Miss Aynk's question, which is to say he responded very positively in our favour. And it was because of us, because we upset the alphabet, that Stepan Dinkin and Eda Dapps began to get to know each other, and, in due course, Stepan and Eda married.

Alva and Irva: matchmakers!

And that is the little story of how we upset the alphabet and at the same time upset our form teacher, Miss Aynk – who was very fond of order, alphabetical or otherwise. In fact, I wonder if she would have preferred never to speak at all and therefore to have left all the words in the dictionary in their correct places.

In class we quickly became academic underachievers, keeping quiet always, huddled close to each other, holding hands under the desk. But sometimes I would be desperate to take part and would raise my free hand even though I didn't know the answer, and when the teacher asked me to speak, and I said nothing, how the class giggled and whooped. In breaks, we would remain at our desk, quietly whispering, and if we were forced into the playground by Miss Aynk or some other unsympathetic teacher, we would shuffle out and quickly find a corner and, pretending to be invisible, long for the class bell to sound. But our fascinated classmates would see us there and would often, at least at first, come over to us. Most of all what fascinated them about us, and what they could never understand, was why we never did things differently, why we always had identical marks in class, why we walked in step, why we scratched our noses, or curled our index fingers around our hair in exactly the same way. They couldn't understand why we were always joined together at the hands, walking in step, as if we were a thing that had four legs, like a horse or a table. Our schoolmates longed for us to do things differently. But we couldn't, not then. It was too early for all that.

And then of course there was Kersty Plint in our class, the daughter of the butcher of Veber Street. Stunning and sexy Kersty Plint, as she would become, was not one of those fey girls who giggle and play with dolls, nor was she the sort of girl whose beauty would in time dictate a certain superior aloofness; rather she was tough and lively and healthy and vindictive. With ease and with relish she would bloody the noses of her classmates, male and female alike, and it was with particular enjoyment that she persecuted us. Most of all Kersty despised our shyness, and the word 'shy' could be attached to almost everything we did. Sticky, sticky adjective. It is with particular distaste that I remember Kersty and her followers, of which there were many, approaching us in the school breaks and pulling us apart and holding us as we wailed at each other across the vast tarmac distance of the playground, begging to be reunited. But Kersty wouldn't leave it at that. She began to see that much fun could be gleaned from torturing us, and she began, with her followers, to enact her Togetherness Exercises, which is the name I gave to Kersty's isolation experiments. She, or one of her followers, would take one of us, Irva or me (she could never tell us one from the other), and hide us somewhere in the school, and then she would have great pleasure in watching the other twin immediately find that location without ever once turning a wrong corner. Or else she would separate us by only a few rooms keeping one in the class-room, for example, and the other in the lavatory, and she would whisper, out of our hearing, to her followers, that at precisely five minutes past eleven she was going to hit one of us, and it was with profound joy that at five minutes past eleven she would note that both twins started crying simultaneously, even though only one of us had been hit. Sometimes she'd have her followers dip one of our heads down a lavatory bowl and pull the chain, and stamp in joy when she heard the report that at the precise time of lavatory dipping the other twin, out of sight and hearing of the lavatory, suddenly took a deep breath and then a moment or so later shook her head as if it were soaking wet. Sometimes she'd simply gawp at the fact that one of us had grown a bruise on a particular place where the other twin had been hit (she never realised that we would often thump each other so that we had identical bruises). But in the end, even Kersty became bored of her Togetherness Exercises and she left us alone.

And of course there was also the business of being tall, which I've avoided up till now, perhaps because it was only at this time that we began to realise it. Father, lest we forget him and his stool perched on top of the table in the kitchen, had given us his tallness genes. We were taller than most of the other children our age, and in time we would grow to the exact loftiness of one hundred and eighty-six centimetres,[7] totally dwarfing our mother, who stood at a mere one hundred and fifty-nine centimetres, or even Grandfather, who we measured one afternoon and found to be one hundred and seventy-three centimetres. When we were girls we wanted this growing of ours to stop. But on we grew, past the hundred-centimetre mark by the age of five, onwards beyond even the hundred-and-forty-centimetre mark by the age of ten, and still we went up further – storeys upon storeys of the sky scrapers of Alva and Irva, which was unfair Irva used to tell me, since all she ever craved for was to be unnoticed, she never wanted to peek out above a crowd, she wanted us to be lost amongst its throng. We finished our great stretching towards the sun at a little over the one-hundred-and-eighty-six-centimetre mark, around the age of seventeen, and from that height, mostly, we looked down on things.

When we were somewhere between the hundred-and hundred-and-fifty-centimetre mark, the two inky boys in the desk behind

---

7. INCIDENTALLY – *For the sake of our visitors not familiar with the metric system of measurement, the twins Alva and Irva Dapps grew to a height of six foot, two inches.*

us in class often used to comment that they were unable to see the blackboard because our large heads were in the way (and when they received poor results in our class they said that our heads, not their own, were to blame). We used to kneel at our bed before sleeping and pray: 'Dear Lord in Heaven, please stop us from growing. Amen.' We tried crouching down, we attempted very studiously to be as small as little Eda, and we believe our marks in class suffered because of the tremendous concentration that this took. But in the end Miss Aynk moved us to a desk right at the back of the school room where we could be more easily invisible, and soon Miss Aynk stopped asking us questions in class.

Eda Dapps came up to us in the playground one day looking sad. She said, 'My mother told me that tall people don't live long, being tall, my mother says, puts too much strain on the heart.' For a moment Eda held hands tightly with us. And then walked away again.

I never wanted to be left alone by our schoolmates. In compensation, I forced Irva to fight me, and so began the days of our historical pugilism. These were attention-seeking fights in which we would hit out at each other just so people would notice us again. At first these fights were just small skirmishes in which only one or two children would notice us but in time they grew into great battles which would only be ended by the arrival of teachers. At first we'd just pull each other's hair a little or slap one another, and only a few children would watch us then. So I decided that we had to be more daring with our fights. Then we'd really punch and bite each other and scrabble about in the gravel and get cuts and bruises. And we were so evenly matched that it was often difficult to tell who had won, and often our fights would be ended by the school bell because otherwise we might have gone on fighting each other, punching and punching until we both collapsed bloody and broken in mutual defeat and mutual victory. These fights of ours, these frantic connections, so amazed people that more and more they began to talk of us. It was joyful for them to watch us, ever amazed as we pulled and spat and beat each other in our agony. People would form circles around us to see us hurting each other, and in that hurt how we became popular! How we were noticed! How they came running as they whispered amongst each other, in classrooms, in lavatories throughout the whole territory of the school: 'Alva and Irva are fighting again, come quickly!' They said to each other, 'They'll kill each other one day, just wait and see they'll really kill each other.' We screamed at each other: 'I'll spill you all over the ground,' or, 'You'll be bald any minute by the time I've finished yanking your hair out,' and, 'I'll stamp your head in,' 'I'll burst your eyes,' 'I'll make earrings of your ears,' 'Your guts: my scarf,' 'Your eyes: my marbles,' 'Your head: my football'. Such words! Such bravery! Such attention! And these fights of ours really had to become increasingly vicious as they continued, those were the rules, we had to hurt each time a little more or they would tire of us, or they would walk away. The teachers separated us, pulled us apart, took little crumbs of gravel from our cuts, and as they bandaged us, ripping up cloths and winding them around bloody knees and elbows, they would ask us why, why did we hurt each other. And we, smiling at each other now, and perhaps even holding hands again, would shrug and demand that we receive the same amount of first aid.

'Please, please, oh please stop,' Mother begged us. 'You must stop this,' Grandfather ordered. 'You will stop,' the teachers announced. They could no longer bear the sight of us in our bandages. Always with a wound here or there. They began to watch us in the playground, it became harder for us to fight, the moment we started, we would be stopped. And then the head-master threatened us, that if we were caught fighting each other ever again, if only once more, we would be separated for good. We would be put in different classes.

With that threat of disconnection, Irva refused to fight me any more and I had to understand that she wanted us to be forever omitted from the lives of everyone else.

After the fights had been stopped, one Saturday afternoon in Grandfather's house on Pult Street (by then we had learnt how to navigate ourselves into Grandfather's district of the city, such explorers we had become), when Grandfather was showing us his matchstick collection yet again, dressed only in his pants and vest and socks and medals, as always, and as he was carving the head off matchsticks with his scalpel, Irva had an exceptionally brilliant idea which I loved her for. And when he gave us a little pocket money (which I always looked after) we went on a journey to the Misons' toy shop on Pilias Street. Mr Misons was there: bad news. He was red-headed, fat and sweaty and smelt of piss a little, which wasn't an encouraging smell, and we were slightly afraid of him and his high-pitched voice. So when he asked us what we wanted we were unable to get it out of us, no matter how hard we tried. 'So tall and so shy,' he muttered, 'unfortunate combination.' But then Mrs Misons came in and that was good news, because she had a way with us. Mrs Misons was on the fat side too, but much less sweaty and she always smelt of talcum, which was an encouraging smell. (And whenever we saw Mrs Misons we were always unable to stop remembering Miss Stott's story of her, we were unable to stop ourselves imagining a pair of male hands upon her breasts, but never were these hands spotted with ginger freckles.) That afternoon Mrs Misons asked us what it was that we wanted, so gently that we wanted to cry with gratitude. (And how guilty we felt afterwards for our thoughts concerning the location of those unfreckled hands.) We pointed at the multicoloured stack of plasticine blocks. Then she whispered to us, 'Which colour?' And we both mouthed, simultaneously, 'Grey.' And then with Irva holding the block of grey plasticine, and me clutching the change, and our other free hands holding each other, we ran not home but to Littsen Street, even though it was a Saturday afternoon.

★ ★ ★

ON THE USEFULNESS OF PLASTICINE BUILDINGS.
1: The Reduction of Troubles. *The Art Museum of Entralla – an essential for all tourists – is a magnificent glass, granite and concrete edifice. Situated on Arsenal Street, it is open from ten o'clock in the morning until six o'clock in the evening. Closed on Mondays and public holidays. Its various highlights include much ancient religious art, especially gold, frescoes and stained glass; an exceptional collection of tapestries, of jewellery and of ceramics from the fifteenth century and numerous oil paintings representing the history of the changing tastes of Entrallans depicted in landscapes, still lives and portraiture. In a guide to world art tourism the author might head various chapters: Michelangelo of Vatican City, Giotto of Assisi, Piero della Francesca of Arezzo, Turner of London, Rodin of Paris, Goya of Madrid, Munch of Christiania (now called Oslo), Klimt of Vienna, Hokusai of Edo (now called Tokyo) and so on and so forth; and if that book were a rigorous and thorough sort of book there would also be one chapter named Chorlin of Entralla. It is this museum, incidentally, and no other, that holds the most comprehensive collection of the works of our celebrated painter Eugin Chorlin, whose canvases most commonly depicted our folk tales and legends, who has been not unfavourably compared to the Flemish (Belgian) painter Pieter Brueghel the Elder. The second floor of this museum, concentrating on more contemporary works, boasts among its treasures four prints by Salvador Dali, a lithograph by Andy Warhol and a napkin signed by Pablo Picasso, and not to be missed are the video installations by the local genius Jorge Bultt (mainly of shots of Entralla and Entrallans, taken at various highly populated locations on a special time-lapse camera, to show us speeded up and rushing about as sun and moon hurriedly trade places). But it is princi-*

pally Galleries 24 and 25 that I would wish you to pay particular attention to.

The first exhibit in Gallery 24, on the right of the entrance, resting on top of a simple wooden plinth, is a model constructed entirely from grey plasticine of a group of buildings that bear a definite resemblance to the school that used to exist on Littsen Street. This model has reduced the size of the school so that its entirety can fit within the palm of a human hand. Careful examination will reward the viewer with the additional knowledge that the plasticine buildings have been pricked all over the surface with an instrument that possesses a sharp point, a needle perhaps or a school compass. These tiny indentations were never to be found on the real structure on which this model is based. If the model was expanded so that its proportions mirrored exactly those of the school, then these indentations would be revealed to be rather more serious than mere pricks of a pin: they would look in fact more like bullet holes, or even the vile gashes caused by mortar shells. If such an enlargement were to take place, or, and rather more simply, if the visitor to the exhibition were to place between his or her naked eyes and the exhibit a magnifying glass, then he or she would assume that the poor school had been the object of some vicious siege. But no siege ever took place on the modern thoroughfare called Littsen Street (named in 1919).

This model, a small monument to wish-fulfilment, is the first recorded insistence of the hopes of the twins being acted out in plasticine and also the first reliable evidence of the twins' skills in the miniaturisation of actual buildings.

★   ★   ★

There were so many school days it's difficult to know what to leave in or what to take out. There was the time when we became ill with the chickenpox (ill at exactly the same time) and the enormous difficulties Irva had in stopping me from scratching my spots because she insisted there should be no markings on us to tell us one from the other. But I don't want to talk about all that nonsense. So I'll skip onwards now until Irva and I became great builders of plasticine, until the time when after school (leaving Mother at the school gates, walking her much slower steps, way behind us – such great strides we had after all) we would come to our attic to construct a city in which we would be happy residents, which was not, certainly not, the city of Entralla. Alvairvalla, as Irva named this place, was a very practicable utopia, and was the first city we built out of plasticine. It was not a very large city, having only forty or fifty buildings.

The important thing for us to remember as we built it was that it was a city for us only, it was built by us and for us, for no one else. Even Mother would not be allowed to enter Alvairvalla. There was only one law in this city which was a huge 'Keep Out' to anyone who wasn't either Irva or me. In fact Irva wrote 'KEEP OUT' on the attic hatch. Mother knocked on the hatch, 'Can't you read?,' Irva said, or, 'You're not blind, are you, Mother, all of a sudden?' Mother was not happy about the city of Alvairvalla and she told us so. She didn't like us always being up in the attic, quietly whispering to each other, she never wanted us to be such private children. She wanted us to share everything with her, but we couldn't, it wasn't natural. We did spend time with Mother when we felt a little sorry for her, sometimes we'd brush her hair for her, sometimes we'd paint her fingernails – though she never went out to see anyone. 'I'm so alone,' she'd say again and again, or, 'Do you love me, Alva? Do you love me, Irva?' We'd tell her yes, but she'd often say, 'You don't, no you don't, I know you don't. You don't have any room for me at all.' Mother wanted to be a citizen of Alvairvalla, but we couldn't allow it. She might have been happy just to be a tourist, just to visit this phenomenon of architectural harmony for a few days, to stay perhaps in one of the two large hotels we built, but Alvairvalla required no tourists to keep its economy functioning and the two citizens of Alvairvalla didn't like people snooping about. In fact, there was another law in the city of Alvairvalla: that should some foreigner ever visit the city, the city would immediately crumble to dust.

Architecturally, Alvairvalla, like Barcelona in Spain, was a city constructed on a grid. It was an ideal city of perfect balance between left and right, north and south, east and west. Each half of the street was a mirror of the other half and each street had an identical street on the other side of the city. There were two of every building – one made by Irva, the other by me. We had two churches, two hotels, two central post offices and no schools. The residential houses were based upon our home in Veber Street, sometimes being a pair of tall versions of the house, sometimes twinned squat versions.

I realise now that the buildings of the city were very unskilfully made, mostly being just oblongs inexpertly carved, but at the time we considered the work to be of unrivalled genius. We were very happy with our city and we always rushed home to see it. It began to govern us. We built a plasticine wall (ten centimetres thick) around the city for protection. We worried about it constantly.

In science class we were taught about the sexual life of wingless *aphidae* (or plant lice), which reproduce asexually (all the baby insects being clones). After that class, during which we noticed that certain of our school fellows had been staring at us, giggling, I pronounced that other people should be allowed to visit the sterile city of Alvairvalla after all. I said the city would die if its two inhabitants never had any children, it would be left empty forever, with perpetually quiet streets, with constantly unoccupied rooms and it would remain in this state, in this void of loneliness because no one except us knew how to find the city, it wasn't on any of the maps anywhere. Alvairvalla, I instructed, would need a third citizen after all, but not Mother, it would have to be a male.

Irva didn't talk to me for a week.

After that silent week, she couldn't bare it any more. She said, 'Yes' and 'All right then.' And so the Quiet Boy entered our history.

I called him the Quiet Boy because he never seemed to speak to anyone. His real name was Girin Lang. He was a year below us at school, and he must have been the most inconspicuous boy in all the world because we didn't notice him for such a long time and generally when we were in the playground we were constantly watching everyone. I used to enjoy watching friendships in the playground, observing them pensively, wondering what they might feel like. And Irva watched me watching friends, but without happiness.

But somehow the Quiet Boy had eluded our gaze before; this Quiet Boy had somehow achieved inconspicuousness. There he was in another corner of the playground, virtually invisible. I became fascinated by him. We would always leave the classroom now in the breaks, just so that I might watch him in the playground. There was so little that was distinguishable about him, except the fact that he wore glasses, which somehow seemed to make him even more hidden, as if his spectacles were a mask. One day we became a little braver, and we managed to be out in the playground before him and positioned ourselves in his particular corner. He came walking towards it, quietly, inconspicuously as always, changing his course now and then to get out of the way of the more noisy and conspicuous boys, who didn't seem to notice him at all, and then as he was almost at the corner he finally saw us. What horror in his little face, what panic. He stood still, stunned for a moment, and then turned around quickly and went back inside the school. I saw him closer that time than I had ever seen him before and I noticed then that one of the lenses of his glasses was gummed up. And then I realised there was something conspicuous about him after all, the boy had a severe squint. One of his eyes saw only Irva, the other only me. In comparison to us, of course, his squint was an amateur in the great circus of conspicuousness, it was a shy and modest and retiring thing. We approached him the next day in the playground, I even spoke to him: 'My sister and I live in Veber Street. We weren't born there, we were born in Saint Mirgarita of Antioch Street, in the hospital that's there. Our father's dead. He died on Napoleon Street. Where do you live?'

When he still refused to speak to us even after our generous words, we followed him all the way to his home which was on Verres Square (way out of our usual route, and I have to admit that twice we became utterly lost as we retraced our way towards home and when I asked people the way they said that they didn't know and that they'd never heard of Veber Street or even of Pilias Street, so in the end, and with Irva frightened and in tears, fearing we'd never find home again, we had to walk all the way to Napoleon Street, which was of course a street that people had heard of, and from there we were able to find home, but always, always it was I, and not Irva, who asked the questions). We followed him for about a week. And I'm sure he noticed us following him, because he'd break into a run just as we were reaching Verres Square and when we turned the corner into the square he wasn't there at all. We knew he lived somewhere on the square but we couldn't be sure which house, we didn't know his exact address. Ah, but we knew someone who would. So the next Saturday morning we went on a trip to Napoleon Street to find that extraordinary man who knew where everybody lived, who was known to us simply as Grandfather. We gave Grandfather Girin's surname and told him that he lived in Verres Square and from that Grandfather was able to work out the precise location of where the elusive fellow was hiding from us: no. 12. And then I said to Grandfather, 'We wish to send him a present.' 'A Valentine?' he asked with a smile. 'No Grandfather,' Irva said in a panic, 'it's April, as you well know.' We showed Grandfather the present. It was a plasticine model just the same as the one we had, of the Littsen Street school though without any scratches on it. Grandfather looked offended. 'You've been modelling,' he said, 'and you didn't tell me.' (Grandfather always wanted us to ask his advice, he felt that it was impossible for us to model without it.) 'I don't recognise the model,' he said, 'What's it of?' But we knew he recognised it. Of course he did. I put it in a cardboard box and put scrunched-up newspaper around it for protection. As I was sealing it up Irva taped a needle on the inside of the box's lid so that that would be the first thing the addressee (a word we learnt from Grandfather) would see and underneath the needle I wrote '© ALVA AND IRVA DAPPS'. 'Why the needle?' Grandfather asked us. When I told him it was to make pock marks on the school, he only went, 'Hem,' and looked disapproving. And so it was sent. And on Tuesday morning it had arrived, but not in time for school. But on Wednesday morning we were certain he had it because he didn't even come out into the playground after class. Well, we were offended of course. But we wouldn't give up, not that easily, though Irva suggested that perhaps we should. And then, mercifully, along came the annual school project to help out.

★   ★   ★

MANDATORY EXCURSION. Lubatkin's Tower. *The history of our city is considered one of the most important subjects for young pupils. Our most celebrated local figure is of course Grand Duke Lubatkin. Lubatkin, for those ignorant of Entralla's magnificent past, was the great warrior who expanded the territory of this region of our country, until eventually other countries joined together and laid siege to our city. (The largest piece of civic sculpture in all Entralla is the impressive equestrian statue of Lubatkin at the foot of Prospect Hill.)*

Look about you, turn around until you see . . . there, at the summit of Prospect Hill, the ruins of the fortress built and protected by Grand Duke Lubatkin. No trolley bus numbers are needed for this excursion – the remaining tower is visible from almost everywhere in the city. Simply use it as your marker and meander through our streets towards it. Climb the two hundred and eighteen steps of Prospect Hill until the tower is reached. Built between

1170 and 1225, it was here that Lubatkin defended the honour of our country, until he too succumbed to death. Not by arrow or by sword but through the horrors of an earthquake. The whole population of our city which was under siege at that time is reported to have died in the quake. It was said afterwards, in the closing section of our oral epic, 'The Entralliad', which every Entrallan knows by heart, that once the earth was still again, 'Neither scream of child, nor wail of woman, neither bark of dog, nor crow of cock, nor any sound but only quiet, eternal quiet, deathly quiet was left within the broken walls of Lubatkin city on Lubatkin hill in Lubatkin land.'

Do take the time to admire the breathtaking view of the city this position offers where all our buildings from the Gothic to the Renaissance to the Baroque, even until the blocks of flats, dreary estates, speak so eloquently of all of the city's days, recent and long since past; these buildings are the cast of characters in the great drama of Entralla. It is even possible to see from this observation post some of the gross damage sustained during the most recent earthquake. Walking down almost any street in the centre of our city it is possible to travel forwards and backwards through so many centuries of architectural taste, but here, on Prospect Hill, all secrets are spilled at once. Here, in this view, the entire history of Entralla is indelibly etched on its wondrous skyline. Has ever a city been so legible? There, look at it, there is the past told in our ancient structures, the present in our modern ones and the future under the shadows of the builders' cranes. Look: history! There is history. As you return to the city, as you are descending the two hundred and eighteen steps of Prospect Hill, imagine that you are accompanied by the shouts and screams of schoolchildren, imagine among those schoolchildren a pair of female twins who seem to be pursuing a bespectacled boy, slightly behind the main group.

★ ★ ★

After a compulsory school trip up Prospect Hill, we were set the task of making something or writing something relating to Grand Duke Lubatkin. This was to take the place of any homework that we might otherwise have been given for three whole weeks. When the weeks were up we were all required, one by one, to ascend the podium in the assembly room and give a brief speech.

Irva and I were absent from the knowledge quest that was ostentatiously exhibiting itself on the large tables of the Central Library on People Street, where boys and girls each attempted to look more studious than the other. What a historic stroking of chins took place in those days as they searched through heavy leather-bound tomes that smelt so sour, and fingered delicate, ancient and misspelt maps of local towns and cities that looked like the efforts of confused men from the mad houses, so little did their work resemble our country's modern settlements. But why were Irva and I not in the library? Where were we acquiring our information? What was our project to be? In the years before, our contribution to the school project had been a miserable inconspicuous thing, timorous and unexceptional, but this year there was something to prove, this year I aimed for us to gain the attention and respect of the Quiet Boy. And so it was that our first victory with plasticine occurred and we came first in school.

* * *

ON THE USEFULNESS OF PLASTICINE BUILDINGS. 2: How to Come First in School. *The second exhibit to be found in Gallery 24 of the Entralla Art Museum is a large model constructed of red plasticine of a historic walled city, within which, on the summit of a hill, are the remains of a fortress. For their entry the twins had created a plasticine model of the architecture of our city built in the time of Grand Duke Lubatkin. But they had not depicted the city as it would have looked through Lubatkin's eyes, rather they had built it as it would be seen in the present were all the buildings erected since Lubatkin's time removed. The* fortress in their model, for example, is exactly how the fortress appears today. But the old wall which used to surround the fortress was no longer clearly visible and only traces of it remain. Occasionally a clump of ancient bricks is seen connected to a more modern building, or more rarely a trench where a part of the wall had been removed. The twins revealed where in the city pieces of the wall are still present and from that were able to show how our city had grown in size since the time of Lubatkin's parental care. During all the research for this model not a single book had been consulted. The twins achieved their knowledge by walking around the old town, carefully observing. All the evidence was there to be found, they simply spent the time to discover it.

This model is certainly in the poorest condition of all the exhibits in Gallery 24. Dust so thick it resembles mould particularly distorts the sad fortress. But worst of all is the length of wall at the southern end of this predominantly empty city. This approximately fifty-centimetre-long imitation of ancient masonry has been flattened out of all shape. If it were possible with minuscule tweezers to remove all hairs and skins of dust, an identifiable print of a child's rather podgy elbow would be found. But the owner of the elbow, a boy called Piter Soffit, was not to blame. He was pushed as the children crowded around the plasticine skeleton of this ancient city. The appearance of Piter Soffit's elbow robbed the city of its beauty and proved in a swift and clumsy moment its heartbreaking fragility. And how cruel it was that its destruction did not make that shattering sound which so alarmingly and worthily brings us to the attention of broken china or glass, how cruel it was that it could be demolished into an illegible lump without so much as a sigh. The teachers were unable to see amongst that scrum of young students who had pushed the boy, though they suspected that it might have been someone called Kersty Plint. Several pupils insisted that in fact it was not Kersty Plint but a boy called Girin Lang, a rumour which the twins never believed.

★　★　★

After the school project a photograph was taken of us standing before our successful model and later that photograph together with one of the whole school and various essays and drawings by other of our fellow schoolmates were put into a metal tube which was sealed at both ends and buried deep in the school grounds. A time capsule. So that other generations of Entrallans, long after our deaths may learn what it was like to be us. Our plasticine victory was safe for centuries to come.

A Love Story Written on the
Ceiling of the Central Train Station

Station Hall

*The hall of our Central Train Station (trolley bus 8 from either
Market or Cathedral Squares, trolley bus 11 from Entralla University), like many another station hall, is far larger than it need
be; even at peak times its immensity is never filled. In the long
afternoons, before a brief fit of activity at five o'clock, the railway customers walk cautiously around the edges, relying heavily*

The Central Train Station

on the emotional support granted by the various periphery estab-
lishments of the ticket office, the waiting room, the lavatories, the
two restaurants (one with waiter service, the other with counter
service selling principally American-style cuisine), before finally
building up the courage to make the distressing dash to their
platform. And yet, one night two school children far from being
frightened by the vastness of this place have felt a freedom here
that they would experience nowhere else in this city.

★   ★   ★

The Quiet Boy, Girin Lang, who we knew secretly wanted to be
with us, continued to avoid us all the time, despite our winning
the first place in school. He very rarely came out into the playground any more and if he did he would always go up to some
other children and speak to them, forcing himself upon their
company. I didn't mind, I could wait. The city of Alvairvalla is a
city of plasticine and of patience.

We continued to follow him to Verres Square. Mother would
inevitably be waiting for us at the school gates but we'd walk past
her: 'We're not coming home, Mother, not yet.' We'd follow the
Quiet Boy all the way to his house on Verres Square, and once we
reached Verres Square, and he'd darted inside his house again,
we'd often sit on benches in the square just looking at his house,
for hours sometimes, just looking. Occasionally we'd see his little
white face peeking through the net curtains on the ground floor,
checking to see if we, his friends, were still there. When we saw
his little face staring at us, we'd stare back at him, our hearts
beating faster and faster, and we'd keep staring at him until his
face disappeared behind the curtains again. He was always the first
one to stop staring. But after a month or so of this following, while
we were sitting in Verres Square, the door of no. 12 opened and
there stood a thin woman with a cigarette, who was the Quiet
Boy's mother, Mrs Lang, looking directly at us and at no one else.

She even walked up to us, she told us to clear off, to leave her son, our friend, alone, to stop terrorising him. Obviously, we said to each other, shaking with nerves, as we returned home, obviously she hadn't understood. We weren't terrorising the Quiet Boy. Hardly that.

The day after we were ushered into the headmaster's office. Grandfather was in the office and so was Mother and so was Mrs Lang, but not the Quiet Boy himself, who she referred to throughout the meeting as 'My Girin' or 'My Little Girin' or 'My Darling Little Girin'. We were told that we were forbidden to follow the Quiet Boy any more, that we had upset him, that we were giving him nightmares, that he would wake up in the night screaming, all because of us. We terrified him, his mother said, we had seen that he was shy and timid and because of this we had gone after him and would never leave him alone. Something had to be done about it.

Mrs Lang said to Mother: 'Your daughters walked straight out of a picture book that frightens children. They should've stayed in that picture book, you should have left them there.' The headmaster told Mrs Lang to calm down, and then with utter strictness he said to us: 'This following/bullying can not continue.'

We were forbidden to go near him ever again; if we were caught following him there'd be great trouble. Verres Square and the Quiet Boy: out of bounds. We must keep our distance at all times. After we left the headmaster's office we had identically red and throbbing right hands from ten strikes each by the headmaster's ruler, which stopped us, for a day, from working with plasticine.

Irva insisted that Alvairvalla didn't need company after all and for a while I agreed with her. We returned to our city and allowed it to grow a little more, adding extra streets for ourselves alone. And it was at this time, as we progressed with our labours, that we discovered it was best, after we had roughly moulded the plasticine into its required proportions, never to touch it with fingers again because fingers always left a mark. And so our plasticine models began to improve as we moved them and shaped them with special plastic and wooden knives which Mr Misons sold in his shop – though these plastic and wooden tools were supposed to be used with clay and not with plasticine.

In any case, very soon people would have more pressing things than us to worry over, very soon our pursuing the Quiet Boy would be forgotten. People's thoughts everywhere would stretch and expand until they were concerned more with planets than with people.

There are many people on this earth who believe the earth to be solid, who trust the surface that they step upon every day and trust it so implicitly that they scarcely even think of it. Terra firma they call it. But the earth is not to be trusted. There is a mighty subterranean engine beneath us and sometimes that engine vibrates and in those vibrations can be heard a roar, a roar of something that will dismiss any faith in that ground beneath our feet. Cracks open and from somewhere down below terror pours out.

In 1742 in Lisbon, the capital of Portugal, an earthquake demolished so much of the beautiful city that town planners considered moving the capital's site completely. In 1976 in Tangshan, People's Republic of China, it is estimated that 350,000 people were killed by an earthquake. On 7 December 1988, 25,000 people were crushed to death in an earthquake in Spitak, Armenia, most of them trapped in public buildings, apartment blocks and schools. Schools.

How we pitied the poor schoolchildren of Spitak, as we sat in our own classroom, together at our shared desk, earnestly regarding the walls and ceiling, trying to seek out cracks. The science master, Mr Irt, the whole of the class, the whole of the city even, were speaking of earthquakes again. There had been a tremor on the earth's surface. Buildings had shaken, a few brick chimneys had collapsed, a few ornaments had jumped down from their shelves to their deaths, but that was all. No serious damage had been caused, and mercifully no one had died. But the aftershocks inside the minds of the people of our city would far outlast the gentle rumbling of that innocent tremor. The younger schoolchildren on Littsen Street, too young perhaps to realise the seriousness of this event, began to scream in the playground, 'An earthquake! An earthquake!,' and even, 'Let's have another,' and then, jumping up and down on the tarmac, they yelled out, 'Come on earth, quake!'

Mr Irt informed our class that seismologists from America had measured the earth tremor. They reported that it was only a minor tremor, that there was still a good deal of stored energy along the fault line on which our city was built. This meant that further earthquakes of a much more serious nature should be expected. When? They could not say. They could guess where and even how violently but not (such is the current failure of the science of seismology) when.

I Ie told us that there was perhaps another way of knowing when an earthquake was about to occur. This method did not involve expensive scientific machinery, this method in fact required only that a person use his eyes. What must he look for? Creatures behaving strangely, fish leaping out of the water, fowls beginning to roost in trees, horses refusing to enter their stables, cats arching their backs and screaming for no obvious reason, dogs beginning to bark and wail though there is no one at the door. Bats, Mr Irt told us, were the most sensitive of all – they began to panic days before the actual quake. Dogs were perhaps the least sensitive, they didn't sense the danger until a few hours before. Humans didn't sense it until it was upon them. He made it clear to our class that the earthquake itself was rarely the direct cause of deaths, but rather it was broken bridges, falling masonry, collapsed buildings, flying glass from broken windows, upturned furniture in houses and offices, fires from broken chimneys or gas leaks, fallen power lines and, most perturbing of all, human panic that did the killing.

Three days after the quake Mr Irt took us all on a school outing. Out of Entralla, actually beyond the city, further than we had ever gone before. He didn't tell us where we were going at first, only that he would show us what damage an earthquake could do. We travelled in the school bus along ever smaller roads, Irva becoming increasingly anxious, feeling homesick, wondering already if we would ever actually see Entralla again. But I felt a joy inside me, as if I could feel myself growing with every moment that we travelled further, I was stretching out over the curved vastness of the globe. 'So much to see,' I said to Irva. 'Open your eyes, look out of the window, look at that! Look at that!' But Irva kept her eyes tight shut. 'How far are we going?' she kept asking. 'How far, Alva, how much further?' And then quieter, 'I don't feel safe, I feel like I'm going to fall any moment, I feel sick.' She was sick when she got off the bus, and I practically had to push her through the door, she didn't want to get off, as if that bus was the only proof that she would be returning home, as if it were the only proof that the city of Entralla still existed. 'I want to go home,' she said, 'I want to go home.' 'Come on, Irva,' I said, 'keep up.' Keep up, I told her, but she couldn't keep up, she never could. Even in those days when she tried, she was always a little way behind, but not out of sight, not yet. Yes, it was certainly this school trip that started the tearing between Irva and me.

The class followed Mr Irt into the woods, Irva holding onto the back of my dress, not daring to look up. And then at last we saw it. There was a name for it, it was called, Mr Irt said, Schimakin. In we went, treading carefully, with handkerchiefs held over our faces (but that would not prevent our snot from coming out in shocking black streaks for days afterwards). What a sombre, wordless school group ours was. Forbidden to enter the angled houses lest they collapse with us inside, we looked in through tilted windows to dark rooms where we imagined we saw something move. Schimakin, with its rusting cars and bicycles, even made some of the class cry.

It was a town without any people in it.

Irva cheered up a little.

★ ★ ★

HIGHLY OPTIONAL EXCURSION 1. A Day Trip to Hell. *Many people from our country will say that there is nowhere called Schimakin, or that Schimakin did exist once but has long since vanished and that no one is quite sure where in our country it was ever actually supposed to be. Many people, they will tell you, have spent their lives looking for Schimakin, and many have been killed in that search, disappearing into the night and leaving no message behind to explain where they have gone. Such are the rumours that surround this abandoned town. Schimakin is absent from our maps, our cartographers have agreed that such an unhappy place should never be allowed to exist. But Schimakin, the Pompeii of our country, does exist, directions can even be provided. Take a bus from the principal bus station, opposite Central Train Station on Terminus Road, heading in the direction of the town of Krilna. En route to Krilna the bus will stop at the village of Ugrick, from Ugrick you must walk in a westerly direction across fields, and, after four kilometres, and behind thick woods, the lost town of Schimakin will be found. No roads lead to that place – they have all been removed, ploughed up, scrubbed clean away. In almost every country there are those wondrous and rare spots titled Places of Natural Beauty, places constantly photographed and made into postcards and exhibited on the carousel stands in newsagents' kiosks nationwide. But there are other, perhaps equally wondrous and hopefully equally rare, spots which exist to compensate, as it were, for those beautiful sites, sites which might be termed, if they were acknowledged (for indeed no newsagent will advertise them), Places of Natural Disaster. Such is Schimakin, an area of high toxicity. One day, deep under Schimakin, the earth became*

81

angry, so angry that a vein of coal two hundred metres beneath the surface ignited and is still alight to this day. How long will it burn? For ever, some say. And what happened to Schimakin when this vein ignited? Gross destruction. The town that was Schimakin began to collapse – the homes, the shops, the colliery fell apart as if it were a place of paper and cardboard. Land implosion; great rifts on the skin of our country. Streets disappeared into the depths and houses and cars and people with them, to this day nobody knows the exact number of miners that were lost. With the collapse of the terrain came the vile smoke for the first time. Never-diminishing pillars of sulphurous gas, more durable seemingly than marble, can still be seen spewing in vertical jets here and there, north, south, east and west on the land that was once Schimakin. When the vein caught, people sitting in the privacy of their lavatories felt that yellow smoke rising up their naked legs and the next moment, still seated at their bowls, they journeyed deep down, pulled cruelly, to a place where humans should never go. People in their sitting rooms felt the earth hiss and saw their brick walls collapse around them. One second they were standing in their homes, the next their bodies lay crippled in the outside air. But not all the buildings of Schimakin went when the ground beneath them rebelled. Some are still there now, neglected, dirty and rotten certainly, but still there – and what strange angles they stand at. Looking at this tilted town today you might at first believe it to be the work of a drunken architect. Look how the buildings list – one bending, but never quite falling, towards the twisted high street, another, its neighbour, leaning far the other way, perhaps to keep this disobeying land somehow in balance. It seems all the buildings of Schimakin have their own minds; perhaps the houses have argued, they face away from each other so. This is Schimakin. No one lives here any more, not even the birds come to visit this stinking place, which smokes and hisses and crackles with its still unspent fury. The sky above it is always darkened. And yet for decades after the disaster some of its people remained, refusing to leave their home; life for them was

Schimakin. They huddled together in their lopsided world until the poisonous fumes made them lopsided too. Even then, those toxic people, unable to abandon their dead, would not leave. In the end they too died, some it is rumoured by throwing themselves deep down into the ignited mine shafts.

* * *

There was a feeling in Entralla then that life was shortly to end, that so many of us were shortly to stop, to be stopped, for ever. Irva and I would look at the crowds on Napoleon Street or the Paulus Boulevard and try to guess which people had been selected for termination. We wandered the city and chose people, at the traffic lights, standing in queues in the Central Post Office, shuffling beneath the large wooden Jesus in the cathedral. How many people in our imagination we parcelled out deaths to in those strange days. Some were quiet deaths, some were noisy and angry and frightened and painful. Now as we walked the old town together, we whispered to each other, 'That one, I think,' or, 'He's going to get it, absolutely,' or, 'She doesn't stand a chance, nope.' We began to clothe the populace of Entralla with an itching mortality that it had perhaps always possessed but which before had been carefully hidden in lonely rooms at three in the morning or behind the windows of hospitals or old people's homes. But these now widespread morbid preoccupations, which were to some utterly defeating, to others brought new feelings of determination and excitement. Suddenly, with each new morning, with each new minute more precious than ever before, came a strange bravery. The quake had tried to teach us that we had little control over ourselves, that we were insignificant and flimsy; but some Entrallans rebelled from that lesson. In those days it was possible to see people wandering about the city suddenly stop dead with a vast smirk on their face, stick out their tongues or raise their fingers in a salute of derision and yell (either down at the ground or up at the sky, depending on whether they were religious or not), filled with this new boldness: 'Give that to your hunchback daughter!'[8] And afterwards they might run off to murder procrastination. Yes, now timid people, who without the earthquake might ever have remained so, proclaimed love to shocked friends or neighbours or burst into their offices and, filled with a glowing inspiration that sped them onwards, became great achievers – freed from their chains of shyness. There was a great sense of doing in the city then; the prostitutes in the Sex District were exhausted; people rushed about visiting friends and family, ending feuds that would otherwise have been exhausted only by funerals; people ate with a voracity that astonished restaurant owners; people danced with a liberation that their bodies had never known before, and perhaps most astonishing of all, when people passed each other in the streets they would often stop and say, 'Good morning,' or, 'How are you?' (even though they may never have met the person before) or, 'What a lovely day' (even though it might have been raining). I was also caught up in this great tsunami of energetic doing and thinking, this need for communication, and I began to sit upright in class.

Before we had always had the junior history teacher. Now, for the first time, old and creased Mr Rinas Riddin, a man who seemed to have lived all history, stepped into our class. This is what he said to us that first morning of his tutelage: 'In order not to slumber in cultural provincialism or spiritual sterility, we are obliged to know everything that happens and everything that has happened in the four corners of the globe.'

We were to discover the world, Mr Riddin proclaimed, and, tugging the class away from our previous history lessons in which our country held a monopoly, the adventure began. We went to war, armed with sharpened pencils and leaking fountain pens.

---

8. INCIDENTALLY – *National expression, English equivalent of 'Put that in your pipe and smoke it'.*

On wintry afternoons, with classroom strip lighting defying the dark outside, we visited Julius Caesar. And in a lighter classroom, as spring began, we watched the Roman Empire burn. Mr Riddin spun the globe on his desk and we visited those places where his index finger, halting the world's rotation, commanded our imaginations. We went to China, to Japan, to Turkey, to Russia, to France, to Britain, to America even.

After Mr Riddin had begun to introduce us to the world, with my insistence, Irva and I would frequently visit the Central Library on People Street. Irva didn't like me studying foreign places, she was jealous of them. But, never bearing to leave me alone, she sat beside me, learning everything I learnt, and somehow, because Irva was with me there, those faraway lands began to lose something of their possibilities. It was as if Irva with her sulky concentration was attempting to turn every city in the world into just another Entralla, to make Paris and Marrakesh and Johannesburg yet more Entrallas only with different names.

We would examine varieties of maps, in the great map room of the library. We'd regard maps of distant cities and I'd wonder to Irva, whispering out those destinations in the hope that saying them would somehow reveal them, 'What goes on in Franz-Joseph Strasse in München, Deutschland?' or 'Who lives in Vytauto Gatve, Vilnius, Lietuva?' or 'What's it like in Via Capo Palinuro in Milano, Italia?' There were maps of modern cities which gave us only hints of real places, maps of cities in ruins – London after its fire of 1666, San Francisco after its 1906 earthquake, Dresden after the 1945 bombing. There were maps of the world ancient and modern, strange early maps in which the initial cartographers had drawn almost everything the wrong size or the wrong shape and had missed out huge land masses altogether, maps of countries, maps (called charts) of seas, maps of sea battles, maps of land wars, maps of long-forgotten empires, maps of geology, maps (called trees) of genealogy, motorway maps, footpath maps, maps showing the populations of the world, poverty maps, temperance maps, maps showing volcanic activity, maps showing flood plains, maps of the human body. And many of them with a little arrow in the top right corner with the letter 'N' above it, for 'North'.

I have always found libraries sexual places. I cannot say why exactly. Perhaps it is because there are so many other people sitting around quietly, and it is a good place to people-watch, and because it is often easier to spend time dreaming up imaginary romances with people just a few desks away from you, who seem so reachable, than to return to the second chapter of a five-hundred-page volume. Perhaps it is because all that studying makes me feel hungry, and that hunger turns to another type of hunger. Perhaps it is because all that silence seems so peculiar and suggestive. Or perhaps it's because of the warmth inside libraries, a warmth which makes so many people fall asleep, sprawled on top of tolerant sentences. Perhaps it's simply watching those people in the intimacy of sleep, which generally they do under covers, behind closed doors, that now I feel I've been given a privileged view of something so private, something that lovers see. In any case, in the library, perhaps simply because of the great exciting mounds of knowledge, I can feel myself warming up. And I enjoyed particularly warm feelings inside the map room, viewing and stroking the colourful surfaces of so many countries, and looking across from our desk to other people, particularly to a certain fair-haired boy, perhaps a year or two younger than Irva and me, who we'd always find somewhere in the library studying maps or guidebooks. But perhaps these sexual feelings of mine had nothing to do with the library at all, perhaps these feelings were just because of the changes that were then going through us, and not only in me but in Irva too, in fact in everyone in our classroom.

The females grew interested first, the males caught up after a while. And many of the males foolishly chose to fall in love with Kersty Plint (whose breasts were the first to arrive, and what full breasts they were), and how she would make them regret it. And we noticed that her many companions now began, more urgently than before, to ape Kersty (in a similar way, I suppose, to how Irva aped me). These girls began to wear their school uniform in the same slovenly way that she did, to laugh as she laughed. When Kersty wore lipstick, they hurriedly bought lipstick; when Kersty arrived one morning with her ears pierced her companions would rush out that afternoon to perforate theirs as well; when Kersty was seen kissing a boy in the school yard, they would hurriedly find themselves an agreeing male and thrust their lips upon his; when Kersty split up with her boyfriend, their boyfriends were summarily dismissed. But these Kersty duplicates were inexact copies with half identities, blurred reflections.

Parts of this new experience were perhaps less new to us than to our classmates. We had practised our first kisses on each other so many years ago, we knew each other under the school uniform so perfectly already. Now with what fascination did we watch each other's bodies changing. We pressed ourselves against each other in scientific comparisons. How extraordinary was this progression of Irva and me. Our nipples decided to enlarge themselves. Beneath them small inexact copies of Prospect Hill began to grow. Our long, thin forms became a fraction more rounded. We began to collect a few hairs between our legs and then more and more, and under our arms as well. Our voices decided they were immature and altered themselves accordingly (but not in the comical way that happened with the males). The upheavals in our bodies made us doubly awkward, long arms and legs always in the way, as if we had too many of each and we were descended not from Dallia and Linas but from a pair of crane flies.

And then I began to bleed. Mother gave me a cotton bag and a purse (to keep with me throughout the day) in which were kept various feminine items which she instructed me in the use of. Irva was jealous, her whole body stiffened with resentment. She could barely move she was in such discomfort, terrified of being left behind. But only a few days later, she was also the happy recipient of an identical cotton bag and purse.

Now, for the first time, I thought it might be good if Irva and I began to spend some moments of each day apart. I began my first attempt to train her away. She could never understand why, she was appalled at this new independence in me, she couldn't conquer it. To begin with it was only for a few isolated minutes that we were separated, then I demanded quarter hours and even half hours. I'd watch her walk away, turning back every few steps to implore me, but I had to be firm, no matter how much I worried, and I did worry then, for both of us – 'It's just for half an hour,' I said, 'only half an hour.' How she crumbled in those half hours when we were apart, bits seemed to fall off her; each time we were reunited there seemed less of her than before. And though I cried honest tears when we were together again, I began to somehow enjoy it all. Whole half hours of terrifying and wonderful loneliness! Such Irvaless moments! Such daring!

There was a boy in our class called Piter Soffit whose principal characteristic was that he longed to be liked. More than anything he wanted to be liked. The more people liked him the happier he felt. When he felt he was liked he positively jerked with happiness. I began to single him out, with Irva dragging behind me, 'Hello Piter, hello Piter.' And he would coyly respond, 'Hello, hello Alva and hello Irva.' 'Would you like to come to our home?,' I asked him one afternoon. 'Really?' he said. 'Yes, I would. Really, really.' Irva didn't want Piter in our home, she begged me not to let him come, so I invited him the next day. 'Very well,' said Irva, 'let him come, but don't show him the city, he doesn't need to see the city, please don't let him see it.' We walked him home in between us (with Mother following behind). I asked him as soon as we were home, 'Would you like to see our city, our own city which we made ourselves?' 'Really?' said Piter. 'Would you show me, really?' I took him up to the attic. I showed him the city, with Irva push-ing him back every now and then, stopping him from getting too close. 'It's beautiful,' he said. 'And to think you made it all your-selves! But where's it of?' he asked. 'It's our city,' said Irva, 'where

Alva and I live, we made it just for us.' 'Oh, I see,' said Piter, 'it's not a real place, it doesn't actually exist.' I stood next to Piter so that we were touching, after a while I began stroking his hair. Piter didn't say anything. 'Do you want to touch me?' I asked. 'Or would you rather touch Irva?' Piter didn't say anything. 'Go on, if you want,' I said, 'we don't mind, you can touch us. He can touch us, can't he Irva?' Piter stayed quiet and didn't move. Nor did Alva. 'Are you shy?' I asked. 'Don't be shy.' And then I stroked him a bit more, and I could hear Piter's faster and faster breathing. And then Piter suddenly started crying. He said through his tears, 'Leave me alone, please, please leave me alone.'

So then I forgot about Piter Soffit and began to concentrate my mind elsewhere. 'We live in Veber Street. We weren't born there, we were born in Saint Mirgarita of Antioch Street, in the hospital that's there. Our father's dead. He died on Napoleon Street. Where do you live?'

That was what I said to the fair-haired boy in the library with the maps and guidebooks, with Irva, anxious Irva, trembling Irva, less and less Irva every day, at my side. The boy looked up at us, very seriously for a few moments, and I began to wonder if he too would demand to be left alone, but then his mouth opened and he spoke, 'I live on Dismas Street. I was born there. My father's not dead, but he doesn't live on Dismas Street, he lives on Cletus Street with his second family. I live with my mother and my sister. They don't understand me. My brother does understand me though, he's older, he's twenty-six, but he lives in Canada now. How about you? Can't you speak?' Those last questions were aimed at Irva, who nodded almost imperceptibly but didn't speak.

His name was August Hirkus and he spent such long hours in the library because he was sure that when he grew up he was going to travel the world. He was solemnly preparing himself for his departure from Entralla which was, he said, 'The most insignificant, piffling, little zilch of a spot, where nothing happens, where everybody speaks one of the most obscure languages in the world just so that the rest of the world will not understand them. But the life of August Hirkus,' he said, 'will not be wasted in such a place. I will be someone, but to be someone,' he said, 'I have to be somewhere first. It's impossible to be someone here,' he said, 'everyone here is a complete no one because this place is an utter nowhere. Yes, first I'll go somewhere, and then, after a while, I'll be someone. What about you?'

We just stared, too amazed at August Hirkus, at this boy who could see his future so clearly. He looked disappointed. 'Christ!' he said. 'A couple of Entrallans, that's what I've got here.' He closed his library books, pushed out his chair, but before he was quite up, and hurriedly, so I wouldn't lose him, I spoke. 'I shall travel to Gaalkacyo, Mudug, Somalia, and to Jinan, Shandong, China. I shall walk down the Avenue Brugmann in Brussels, and the Avenue Insurgentes in Mexico City. And Ramses Street in Cairo. And the Zagorodnyy Prospekt in Saint Petersburg. And the Khiaban-e Akbarabad in Tehran. And Waterworks Road in Brisbane.'

I could have gone on. I was only just beginning. 'All right,' he said, 'you can come.' We went outside to the library steps – Irva came too, even though she wasn't invited – and we smoked our first cigarette (sharing one of August's cigarettes between us, coughing and smiling). That was how it started, soon we spent more and more time with August, who we learnt was, or so he told us, a difficult child. He was frequently getting into trouble, frequently arguing with his mother, and almost always ignoring his sister who was not a difficult child, who was in fact a very easy child, who made her mother proud, who was swimming captain at her school, who knew many different chunks of the Bible off by heart, and came top in divinity, who had many friends and a voice that was considered exceptional. August, however, rarely sang and could barely swim, he had no interest in the Bible (except to hide his sister's), he had no friends at school. He told us how he would be rude to the teachers in the classroom, that he would ask questions that deliberately embarrassed them. He rarely saw his father, except when he wanted money. He frequently skipped class and was on occasions caught shoplifting; once he was seen dropping stones from a bridge onto a train track. He liked to buy canisters of car paint and scrub out street signs and whenever the word 'ENTRALLA' appeared on posters or signs throughout the city he would write above it the word 'FOR' and beneath it the words 'READ NOWHERE'. He asked us if we'd seen his graffitied signs, we nodded even though we'd never seen them. The Entrallan police, August told us, had a file with his name written on it, just about him, a file that, he said, grew thicker almost every day. I loved him! I'd do anything for him, he was the most astounding person I had ever met. I'd spend hours with August searching through maps and travel guides, sitting so close together, with Irva, a table away, watching us. August and I would have long discussions on the various merits or downfalls of certain famous hotels throughout the world. And it was whilst we were sitting on the marble steps of the Central Library that August said he was able to tell us apart, that it was easy to do so, and in the future whenever we tested him, he always got it right. Irva, he said, was always the one with the anxious expression. And how that seemed to increase the anxiousness upon her face, to burn it there.

August and I would touch all the time. We'd mock-fight each other. And I'd long for him to kiss me but he never did. I kissed him on the arm one evening, on the library steps, with Irva sitting a few steps behind. I gave him a love bite, a big purple island on his salty skin. (That night Irva gave me a love bite too, also on my left arm, even though I never asked for one.)

More and more Irva would begin to fall behind. She wanted to stay with us, but we couldn't bear to have her there all the time, she got in the way, she crowded us, she couldn't keep up but she was always somewhere, just behind us, lagging away, saying, 'Can I come too? Can I come? Can I?' I so loved her, of course I always loved her, but then, in those days, I loved hurting her too. I'd whisper to her with a confident smile, 'Who are you Irva? Will you please tell me who you are because, to me, it doesn't seem you're anyone at all, not really.' Sometimes walking with August, I'd suddenly stop, turn around on the pavement, march the few steps back to where Irva was and say, 'Go home, Irva, go home,' as if it were only a dog and not my sister who was following us. Once we all went to the McDonald's restaurant on the Paulus Boulevard. I sat her down at a table, and August and I went to buy our food. She wanted to come with us, but I insisted she guard the table, and instead of buying food August and I simply walked out of the back entrance onto Toller Street and we were free, we were running away, laughing at our ingeniousness. Two hours later we happened to be walking down the Paulus Boulevard and we looked through the windows of McDonald's, and there was Irva, still there, waiting, still seated at the table.

Those days were the great days of my wildness. I started to miss class. August and I would spend school mornings and afternoons wandering from shop to shop, stealing little things that we had no real use for. Sometimes we'd run about the train station together, or squeeze ourselves inside the passport photograph cubicle in the station hall and make grimaces for the camera and afterwards out would plop four photographs of squashed and happy friends, so close together in such a small space. And sometimes on those days as we hurtled through the city we'd catch Irva somewhere behind us, just a few buildings away. And then came the nights when August and I used to buy car paint and spray onto brick walls the messages, 'FINLAND, LAND OF LAKES', or, 'ITALY: CULTURE AND CHIANTI', or, 'FIND ADVENTURE IN ALASKA'.

And every night when I got home I'd tell Irva all about my fresh experiences until she cried.

It was on one of those days of our earliest separation that I went up to the attic to find the city of Alvairvalla in ruins. Irva had smashed it. There were visible imprints of her misery all over the city, misshapen houses lay winded, sprawled now off the pitted streets, imprints of her fists visible in their distorted faces. Some buildings had been pulled out of the city and scraped for long centimetres flat against the walls, or were on the floor covered with the stamp of Irva's shoes. I could see on the ruined streets great gashes in the plasticine from where Irva's clawed hands had scratched.

Poor Irva, I thought, how sad.

Once August and I visited the Civic Bakery, which was the place where August's father worked, but we didn't go to visit him, instead we went to visit the great Bakery Clock Tower and to look on Entralla from above, and August from that great height took out his willy and pissed down upon the city and I laughed so much my giggles became cackles. And down below on the ground was Irva. Did she wonder that day why it began to rain a little, even though there were no clouds in the sky?[9]

---

9. SITES OF INTEREST. Bread Square. *The centre point of Bread Square is the spot where some of our adolescent children like to pass their expansive and unprofitable time. It is not a bench that they congregate around or a statue or even a war memorial, but an abandoned piece of architecture. See how lovingly they prop their bicycles against the structure's walls, see how lovingly they clamber over the structure, see how lovingly they clamber over each other whilst inside the structure. It is a place of teenage violence and friendship and love. At night, under this roof, amidst empty bottles of beer, how many boys and girls have experienced their first carnal adventures? They have defaced the walls with their names, with their declarations of love, both inside and outside; they have drawn crude anatomical chalk drawings (principally depicting the male and female sex organs) which writhe and tumble their way across the walls of the tiny room at the high-est point of this ruin. But what is this solitary scrap of a building at the centre point of this city square, which has become a home to all the anxiety and muscles and hopes and lies and crushes and betrayals of the vast soapopera of adolescent yearning? It is the skeleton of the bakery clock tower. Bread Square, named since the earthquake – when so*

Mother, who by then must have returned to work at the Central Post Office, began to be ruled again by her private terrors. She would still go to the school gates and often she'd be waiting there until the entire school had left Littsen Street and the gates were even closed up for the night, and still she wouldn't have seen us because neither I nor Irva would have gone to school all that day. And then more and more often Grandfather would be waiting at home when we finally returned, me first and then Irva always a few minutes behind, always with such a strange expression on her face. Grandfather would try to frighten us with gloomy predictions of our future lives and sometimes we'd be shown letters from school and sometimes a teacher would come and I'd hear Mother saying, 'I don't understand them . . . they barely talk to me any more . . . they won't talk to me.' But I didn't care about all those people. They were merely Entrallans. They didn't count.

On the station steps I showed August the extraordinary piece of paper I had ripped from a library book when no one was looking, just for him. Grand Central Station, New York, more like a palace than a train station. But the cerulean blue ceiling, that was the

---

many names were changed – was where my father used daily to work. Before there had been no square on this spot, the vast civic bakery had filled it entirely, its warm, yeasty smell had stretched its goodness around the neighbouring streets, comforting them. But the bakery and many of the bakers inside it were destroyed one July 16th. Twisted girders, ruptured machinery, mounds of brickwork, were all that remained but the clock tower at the top of the building, though now standing at a strange dislocated angle, survived virtually intact. When the building was set to be completely demolished, the clock tower out of a whim of the city reconstructors was removed from the top of the crumpled body and – once the exhausted corpse of the bakery had been tugged away, and the ground levelled and made into a square – found its place as a monument to our earthquake. It no longer registered time, the mechanism had failed, cogs had twisted, springs had snapped. The broken timepiece was removed, with only the blank clock face remaining.

most beautiful thing, spotted with the celestial globe. The stars, all the signs of the zodiac, but not just the stars, many of which were lit up by tiny bulbs, there were also outlines of the people and the things the stars were named after. Then August had his idea: 'Why don't we paint the stars on the ceiling of our train station?' 'Do you think we could?,' I asked. He said, 'I don't see why not.' 'Wouldn't they stop us, surely they would?' 'Not if they don't know, not if we paint it at night when the station's closed and locked up.'

That night, when the station was cleared, when the station gates were bolted, August and I arrived holding a pot of white emulsion paint and two brushes. There was a small side gate and then a turnstile, which we climbed over. And then we were inside the train station. And so our work could begin. We climbed way up a metal ladder bolted onto the wall and we sat with our feet dangling on one of the metal girders that supported the ceiling. It was like sitting on the ribs of a huge man, a great skeleton made of iron. We were alone in the station, it felt like alone in the world, only me and August and the pigeons trying to sleep. There was so much mess on those metal rafters, soot and dirt and rust and the pigeons had claimed them as if they were built for them alone; there were feathers and shit everywhere. We carefully stood up, balancing ourselves with one another, we took our paint brushes and using the photograph of that famous ceiling in New York as our guide we began to paint. The paint went everywhere, dripped all over us, dripped on the pigeons' shit, dripped on the pigeons, as if it were our own shit and we, much bigger birds, were shitting on them. It dripped all the way down to the station hall too, we heard it fall, sounds that seemed to us like a bum being smacked (a warning, perhaps, of what was to come). August's coat had great streaks down it, and so did his hair and so did his face. The station ceiling wasn't easy to paint, it was so filthy up there that the paint had to be laid on thickly or no marks would be made, and the brushes soon became gunked up. Our constellations weren't accurate. They were too bunched up and all in a tiny part of the station ceiling. But, all the same, we were very proud of our work.[10]

We were up there for perhaps an hour, possibly more, maybe two, moving carefully between the metal ribbing, positioning white dots. It would probably have been better if one of us had stayed down below and called out directions, since once back on the hall floor we could see just how inaccurate our daubing was. But I'm glad we were both up there, there was something so good about getting dirty together. When we did finally descend exhausted, we stood in the centre of the hall, looking up at our non-fluorescent stars, visible only because of the lights of the lavatory signs and the Coca-Cola machines which were always lit up, and looking down at the mess we'd made on the floor. Such a huge place all for us. And we pulled the drying paint out of each other's hair. And then we began to pull off our paint-covered clothes. And to kiss each other everywhere, all over.

------

10. SITES OF INTEREST. The Central Train Station ceiling. *If you walk towards the right-hand side of the station, towards the ticket office, and look upwards, you might be able to catch a glimpse of what was created one late spring night. I cannot guarantee, however, that you will be able to see our work, for it is many years since we took our position on the great rusty vaulting of the Central Train Station, a dangerous enterprise, and much dirt has rushed up to the ceiling since to hide our inexpertly drawn celestial map. You may, though, if you stay there long enough, long enough perhaps to feel your neck painfully aching, you may, if you are patient, and with your eyes squinted in an effort to concentrate their search, you may see a few white, off-white certainly, corrupted white, patches, less dirty than the rest of that section of the ceiling, blotches just a little whiter than their neighbours. You may be able to see a few of those. For those barely discernible smudges are all that remain of our courageous project, and now, far from reading the night's sky on the ceiling of the hall of our Central Train Station, you will perhaps, and only perhaps, be able to see an uncertain and lonely universe with only one or two fading stars flickering vaguely in the selfish darkness, and even these you cannot really be certain to have seen. But once, believe me, they were there. Once you had only to look up to see a squashed Aries, a surely smashed Plough, and the Gemini cramped close together.*

That night something else moved in the darkness. Someone else was there. But we didn't hear anything then, we were completely deaf, too busy with ourselves to hear. But as August and I kissed, and as we pressed our naked bellies against each other, then, at that moment, just then, when I felt that August and I were all that existed in the world, yes, just then, just at that moment, there was a scream from the darkness, a wail of such enormous unhappiness, a cry of such absolute misery and hurting, so loud it brought the night-watchman running.

The night-watchman, a man of supreme joylessness, didn't like what he found in his station hall. Perhaps he might have been more understanding if there hadn't been paint everywhere. But the combination upset him. There was too great an intimacy on the station floor and too much mess that went with it. He could not allow it to remain there, it was against the rules, there were too many people where he expected and wanted none. He shone his torch into us, rasping obscenities under his breath, he called the police on his radio, he stood by us with his torch until the police came.

The police, tired and angry, muttered and grimaced and ordered us to scrub the paint from the floor. But they never looked upwards, they never looked at the ceiling, never imagined that we'd been up there, August and I, and they never looked around the hall either to see if someone else might be hiding.

When we'd finished cleaning they took us to the police station, silent and guilty now and ashamed, even August was shaken for once, so shy suddenly that it was impossible for us to look at one another, because a shared look then might have shattered our spines.

August and I waited on a bench screwed into the ground, we waited for such a long time, not speaking to each other until, finally, I was ordered into an office.

A little desk and a little man who looked bored and sad. He

gave me a long talk which came with a warning, only a warning for me because I had never done anything wrong before, a warning and a fine. I asked him what they were going to do with August, whether they were going to take him away. He said it didn't concern me. When I left the office August was no longer there. His position on the bench had been taken by Grandfather.

Grandfather had come to pick me up in one of the post office vans. He didn't say anything, he just drove, as if it were a package and not a person beside him. Poor Grandfather, he must have been thinking about those panties he found one morning on the post office steps years back, he must have been thinking that somehow these two events were connected. Poor Grandfather, he was always happier with matchsticks than with people.

Irva had come home hours ago.

For a week after the Train Station Adventure I was forced in my disgrace to remain home. Grandfather came to Veber Street just to see me, to tell me that August had gone away to live in Canada. 'Which is all for the best,' he said, 'since neither his parents nor his school can control him. He's gone away to start a new life with his brother. He shan't be coming back.' 'But,' I protested, 'that can't be, it isn't true. He told me that he'd never go without me. He promised me. He promised.' 'Well,' said Grandfather, 'he lied then, didn't he?'

We hadn't even measured him. How many centimetres made up August?

I stole a map of Canada from the map shop on Donkey Street, I slept at night with that map underneath me. Irva lay next to me with her eyes open. I said in my sleep, 'Niagara Falls, Lake Ontario, Quebec, Toronto, Newfoundland.'

'I'm going away,' I kept saying to Irva. 'I'm going away.'

She stopped talking to me and I never went anywhere.

I needed to mark myself from her, I wanted there to be a sign, something to prove that I had experienced other things, something to stop the sameness. I wanted everyone to see that there was such a difference between Irva and me. I wanted everyone to know.

We had reached the age of sixteen, it was time for our class to split and, at the end of the school year, for some students to prepare themselves for further learning, and beyond that for university, and for others to set out into that place termed by uninspired adults the Real World. The lower half of the class was dismissed to seek employment. Irva and I were to work in the post office, in positions found for us by Grandfather, not serving customers in the hall of the Central Post Office but instead delivering letters about the city.

On one of our final days at the educational establishment on Littsen Street, during one of the breaks between lessons, I took myself into the lavatory with my school compass. Fifteen minutes later, five minutes into the next lesson, I calmly walked into the classroom and sat down at our desk.

The whole class stared at me, the teacher called for the head-master, and Irva, my neighbour, moved away. I had drawn on my forehead with the point of my compass, deep into my skin. Tearing into myself with that sharp metal point. My blood, sister blood to her blood, dripped down my face. But that blood did not stop the classroom from reading what I had etched there: a vertical arrow pointing upwards and above that the letter 'N', for 'North'.

N
↑

As if I were a compass.
As if you would never get lost as long as you had me with you.
Now everyone could tell us apart.

Interlude 2

Lunch

THE INTERNATIONAL WORLD HOTEL
Paulus Boulevard 16–24   Open 12:00–24:00   Tel. 316 22 25

Within the International World Hotel is the Piccolo Mondo Bistro. This slightly shabby eatery has plenty of decorations to occupy your time whilst waiting for the service, which is exceptionally friendly whilst not always swift. Though the ceiling is crumbling, we have sincere assurances that it is never likely to fall into your plate. The restaurant boasts views onto the much rebuilt side of

The International World Hotel

the Paulus Boulevard. *Specialising in our national cuisine, the very imaginative menu can cater to most tastes but be warned: oversized portions. Menus in English. No reservations required if seen holding a copy of* Alva & Irva, the Twins who Saved a City; *otherwise recommended.*

★   ★   ★

The World Hotel, *sometimes referred to tautologically as the International World Hotel, is the largest and most celebrated hotel in our city, though it is not necessarily the most comfortable. Situated on one of our main thoroughfares, the Paulus Boulevard – accessed from trolley buses at all the major city squares with its great width and tall symmetrical buildings, was part of the Haussmannisation of our city which took place after our most recent earthquake. On the Paulus Boulevard (our version of the Champs-Elysées in Paris, Oxford Street in London, Unter den Linden in Berlin) we have clothes shops, including, for example, a GAP; we have jewellery and watch shops – which sell merchandise from such prestigious companies as Rolex; we have large pharmacies which sell products of such brands as L'Oréal, Christian Dior and Laboratoires Garnier; and also we have that most popular and dependable and truly international of culinary establishments, McDonald's.*

You will find the World Hotel by finding the McDonald's restaurant. The restaurant is extremely visible; the hotel, at least at first, is not. The World Hotel, formerly the Paulus Hotel, changed its name shortly after our earthquake, when many buildings had their names changed just to strengthen a feeling of newness and of hope. There was even a man on J. F. Kennedy Street called Mindus who suddenly and without any warning insisted he was now to be called Mark. Just so he felt new. A most confusing business. But as far as the hotel was concerned, the name changing was made for professional reasons. It was felt that the moment the hotel mentioned the word 'World' on its stationery, men and women from every conceivable country would suddenly come rushing through its swivel doors. They didn't. These things take time. There is a mumbled rumour that a Holiday Inn wishes to place itself in a very prize position overlooking Ventis Park, but I am unable to confirm this matter for you – perhaps if such a presence were to arrive here then the World Hotel would quickly lose what shifting populations it so tenuously possesses. When the World Hotel first became the World Hotel they flew flags of many countries from its grand terrace (now the second storey of the expanding McDonald's restaurant). Truly, the people were supposed to gasp, this was an international place. The people stared at those flags. And the longer they stared the more they worried – didn't the French flag have vertical and not horizontal stripes; did the American flag have enough stars; did the Australian flag really have a kangaroo in its centre? And then they realised that the flags were home-made, bold but ersatz productions: they were sheets from the old Paulus Hotel, which even had the word 'Paulus' stitched into them, cut up and sprayed with car paint.

In between McDonald's and a large pharmacy are two marble urns growing plastic orchids and in between the urns is a revolving door. Please enter the World Hotel, a building in the Modernist style constructed in 1938–9.

The Piccolo Mondo Bistro. *Inside the lobby with its marble-tiled flooring, with its pillars shaped with moulded plaster into palm trees, with its red flock wallpapered walls (with proud blisters), with its threadbare leather sofas (whose visible springs aim any day to launch themselves), with its formica-topped tables (on which rest glass ashtrays as big as sinks), is a bellboy, in his sixties, puffing on an anorexic cigar, willing to take you up to the fourth floor where the Piccolo Mondo is to be found. Take the opportunity, as you cross the large hallway, to view the reception desk with its vast, heavy, leather-bound ledger, and behind that the black plastic notice board on which the prices of rooms are carefully listed with white plastic click-in numbers. Please note* that there are two different prices, one for nationals, one for foreigners. Note also the wall of keys behind the desk. Two hundred little wooden niches. Imagine what rendezvous of secret love, what fumblings of purchased love, what loveless loneliness have rumpled the sheets of the World Hotel and imagine what variety of dreams have woken so many guests to the black night, which always seems darker still inside those various allotted spaces. One human life (the bastard daughter of some miserable American heiress) even arrived on the third floor in room 327 and seven lives over many years have departed in these beds, forever ignorant of the knocking of the maid's forceful hand, with lonely, polished shoes waiting patiently outside. But if all these rooms have one thing in common it is that they are not home, they are mere temporary lodgings with unfamiliar, unfriendly beds. Like Venice with its transitory population of tourists, the inhabitants here are always changing. Like Venice, no one stays except the staff. But like the frowning Ezra Pound who remained in that ancient and rotting Italian gone-to-seed Disneyland, here too there is an exception, for on the fifth floor, in rooms with a balcony over-looking the city, lives the old retired former mayor of our country, forever dictating to his resourceful secretary the memories, always professional, never personal, of his years in office. Ambras Cetts, suite 500. He never leaves his rooms. People come and people go but not Ambras Cetts, cancer patient. His travels, beyond excursions to the lavatory, to his bedroom, bathroom, sitting room, balcony, have ended.

Enter the lift. Your copy of this history will be all the information required for the bellboy, still enjoying his cigar, to launch you to this excellent bistro, by pressing with one of his yellowed fingers the button numbered '4'.

I cannot say exactly why the restaurant was misleadingly named Piccolo Mondo, for its Italian wording would indicate a place celebrated for pasta or pizzas which it is not especially, though both are available. It was surely named thus to add to the international flavour of the place; it might just as easily have been called *La Petite Monde* or even *Die Kleine Welt* or *The Little World*, but for some reason the Italian version was preferred. The first thing that you will notice about the restaurant, beyond its thirty round tables all with well-starched tablecloths, are the various ornaments that clutter the ledge which runs around three-quarters of this large room. On this ledge are nearly three hundred items of international treasure, among them: a pink rubber Michelangelo's David; a three-dimensional terracotta version of Leonardo da Vinci's Last Supper; a plastic gondola with flashing lights; a small, framed photograph of the Mona Lisa that winks at you as you move across the room; a bottle of shampoo shaped as the Virgin whose head, when turned anti-clockwise, opens the bottle; a brass Eiffel Tower that plays the Marseillaise when turned upside down; a candle in the shape of the Arc de Triomph; a clockwork tin Napoleon; a pair of dolls of Prince Charles and Princess Diana; a miniature Brandenburg Gate; various small busts of Lenin, Stalin, Ho Chi Minh . . . and so on and so forth. There are numerous buildings beneath transparent plastic domes which if shaken produce a 'snow storm' effect, representing the Tower of London, Mount Rushmore, Saint Peter's in Rome; there is even a small plastic replica of Lubatkin's Tower in this style (but more of that later).

The wall behind the bar is papered with banknotes from some seventy different countries, illustrations of so many men and women famous in so many different lands; a version of the History of the World could be made simply by listing their various contributions. The remaining wall space is decorated with large photographs of buildings from our city only, by far the largest representing the World Hotel (a black and white photograph taken before the arrival of the McDonald's establishment).

Allow yourself to be drawn towards the table indicated by your waiter and once seated take your time to peruse the menu, the special menu provided for those bearing the volume **Alva & Irva, the Twins who Saved a City**, *written in English; a kind of English at least, in which 'cruditées', for example, are translated* as 'assorted pigments'. But I am sure the intelligent among you will soon, and with some delight, be capable of extracting the true identities of all the extraordinary offerings. There is no 10 per cent reduction here, but the folded laminated cardboard in front of you should more than compensate for that fact. The special menu is divided into two. The left-hand section is titled 'Piccolo Mondo according to Irva Dapps'; the right-hand section 'Grando Mondo according to Alva Dapps'. The special menu for those holders of Alva & Irva, the Twins who Saved a City is given over to the particular culinary preferences of the two subjects of this history. From this menu you will learn that Irva preferred to eat only food traditional to our country and that Alva preferred to eat only food traditional to other countries. While in the entrées section, for example, you will observe that Irva is more than happy to eat beetroot and onion soup topped with sour cream (it is in fact the only option), Alva's more eclectic desires range from calamares, to salade niçoise, to spring rolls, to prawn cocktail, to roasted goat's cheese, to various antipasti, to chicken samosas, to fried cur- ried chicken livers, to moules marinière. I would suggest varying your choice to include at least one item from each side of the menu so that you are, during those brief moments when the food enters your mouth, tasting what it was that Alva and Irva loved to taste, for then as you masticate you will have a more total experience of the Dapps twins. If you are having problems choosing, I would like to alert you to a few recommendations to be found on the menu's reverse and made by foreign visitors who have been pleased to add their suggestions. 'The salads at the Piccolo Mondo are far larger than the salads in any other of the local restaurants.' – Sukrita Paul Kumar, Delhi, India. 'The pigs' trotters with mushed corn are so good that you'll return to the city just to taste them again.' – Asdis Thorhalsdottir, Reykjavik, Iceland. 'The bread and butter pudding is better than any I've tasted at home, better even than my mum's, but don't tell her that.' – Isadora Carter, London, Great Britain. Choose. Eat. And, as the Americans say, enjoy. Do not be put off by the mobile phone disturbances of the nouveau riche males entertaining their youthful, beautiful, but predominantly silent, female companions. These men make up most of the custom here.

   After you have eaten, I advise the participation of some coffee with which both Alva and Irva, reuniting for once, would have completed their meal. Or perhaps even a glass of our local Lubatkin brandy, 50 per cent proof.

Part Three

THE WORLD & OUR CITY

A Postwoman from Our City
Once Travelled the World
without ever Leaving Our City

Arsenal Street

Arsenal Street, leading directly off Market Square (see map) is one of the oldest streets of Entralla. Its once cobbled surface may have given way to the more modern asphalt, but much of its history still remains – many of its buildings proclaim dates above

Pig Mikel's Tattoo Parlour

their old stone portals in Roman numerals. Lubatkin's great store
of bygone weaponry once stood on this site; it is long gone but a
reminder of its existence can be found in the centre of the street
where a portion of its ancient wall still resides and continues to
possess two great iron rings from which horses used to be tethered.
Where people once parked their horses, taxis now await business,
a testament to the fact that human beings are still, through so
many centuries, interested in the phenomenon of travel. On
Arsenal Street, just across the street from Market Square, is a
small dingy shop. There is a dim red word, electrically lit, that
flashes on and off, unenthusiastically labelling the purpose of
these premises: 'TATTOO'. This then is a tattoo parlour and it is
here that Mr Pig Mikel rules. But Mr Mikel is no longer able to
continue his skilled profession, that is left to his two apprentices
who he barks commands at, forever unhappy with their excellent
work. Time has spoilt Mr Mikel's eyesight, misshapen his back,
and made his fingers dance perpetually.

★ ★ ★

Above and below. High and low. Everywhere and nowhere.
Upside and downside. Forwards and backwards. Upwards and
downwards. Outwards ·and inwards. Outside and inside. Over
and under. Alva and Irva.

At first we didn't really notice the great changes in her. She had a
cold certainly but there was every expectation that she'd be better
soon. When she didn't speak we assumed she would in time, that
she'd grow tired of not speaking; that her speaking would come
back. And after a week of her not speaking we began to get used
to it, we grew accustomed to this Irva of ours who didn't speak.
It became perfectly ordinary for us to have this silent Irva in our
home. We didn't feel we were neglecting her, just that she had
chosen to be silent. It was her decision. In time she'd grow bored
of it. We'd wait her out. And did they ever notice, I wonder, that

I spoke now far more than usual, that I was speaking, so it seemed to me, for two?

And with the silence there was the other thing, which took us a while to understand. My sister had decided never to leave home again. Anything beyond home was out of reach for her, Mexico or Pilias Street, Tasmania or Cathedral Square, Manila or the Public Library were all the same distance away; an insuperable distance that she could not dare to travel. She was happy where she was, why move? In the beginning, Mother and Grandfather even encouraged her to stay at home, she had a cold after all. Better to sit quietly at home. Better to stay quiet and sit still, and wait peacefully for recovery. So for a while no one commented that she hadn't been outside. And nobody commented that I was out more than usual, that I was busy rushing about the city, that I couldn't keep still.

I had marked myself with my school compass, I had deliberately separated myself from Irva. And Irva almost immediately had started sneezing. Then she got the shivers. Then she stayed at home. Then she stopped speaking.

They gave her some pills, she never went anywhere around the house without her bottle of pills, their rattling always betraying a change in her location, but mostly she would be found scrunched up on her bed facing the wall. Her capacity for sleep in those days was enormous.

I was ordered to sleep in the next-door bedroom. Mother gathered up my things, one half of everything inside the room, an identical half, an exact half, and deposited it in the spare room. A stranger visiting our house that day could be forgiven, as the tour of our home progressed, for believing that he had seen the same room twice. Irva tried to keep back some of my objects by hiding them under the bed or in our old wardrobe or by clinging to them. Mother was ruthless. Mother vacuumed the room, and dusted thoroughly. And so Irva was left in her Irva territory, existing only of Irva. It was for the good, Mother told her, imitating Grandfather, when she wailed. I closed the door to my new bedroom, I sat on my bed. All this is mine, I thought, only mine, I shan't allow anyone else inside. 'This,' I whispered, looking about me, 'is private property.' And I vowed I'd change and expand the contents of my little kingdom until it in no way resembled the contents of that Irva-land so close by. As I sat in my room that day I thought of August Hirkus in some equivalent room far away in Canada.

After Mother divided our property, and set us Berlin-like, in different worlds, Grandfather, as some kind of privileged ambassador, wandered throughout the house, not commenting on the great change, but noticing it profoundly. He tried to cheer things along with his onwards-onwardsness, but it never worked. And he could never bear to stay for very long. He tried to make light of the healing scab on my forehead, saying it was very helpful. Looking at the arrow pointing at the letter 'N', he would comment, 'Alva Dapps, this way up'. Or sometimes he would call me 'North' and Irva 'South'. But nobody even smiled and Mother opened the box of kitchen matches and began to snap one matchstick after another in half, so he soon got the message. So he soon shut up. So he soon went away again. But he would always leave by smiling at me and saying, 'Alva, it'll soon be September and then you'll begin at the post office. In the meantime enjoy your holiday.' But I never wanted that holiday, and when I told Grandfather I'd happily begin work immediately, he shook his head and told me I'd better wait. 'Besides,' he said, 'by September that scar will be barely visible.'

In those days I was experiencing my new independence. As I grew so Irva faded. The north sign had confirmed how fundamentally different I was from her. And I did not wish the wound to go away. Irva began to wear a woollen hat to cover her forehead. I began to pin my hair back with a multitude of hairclips. Sometimes Irva would fold up sheets of loo paper and tape them with plasters to her forehead, but these were half-hearted efforts which fooled no one. When a scab was formed I would painfully reopen it in the privacy of the bathroom. I clung desperately to my new independence. And it was only after my fourth of fifth visit to the doctor, with an insistent and distressed mother in the lead and with myself in tow, that the doctor said the following comforting truth, 'I don't know what it is that you're trying to do, young lady. If you'd left your scab to heal naturally there'd hardly be a mark on your forehead, but now, and because of your protracted vandalism, you are sure to have a scar there for the rest of your life. I hope you're proud of yourself.'

Thank you, doctor. I was. And then I left my forehead to heal.

Meanwhile, outside of the listless house, 27 Veber Street, it was hot, hopeful, sexy, thirsty summer. And out I went, out into new days!

On Veber Street, on Sundays, I would always see the heavy man Jonas Lutt, the long-distance lorry driver who lived at no. 15, washing his car. I always looked out for Jonas's T-shirts. Sometimes he would wear one which said, in German, 'MUSEUM FÜR VÖLKERKUNDE, HAMBURG', or else, in Polish, 'ZAMEK KRÓLEWSKI, WARSZAWA', or else, in English, 'DOVER BY NIGHT', he had such a collection of T-shirts! I would stop to talk to Jonas every Sunday. It is true of many people that even when you've hardly met them they already begin telling you their life stories, as if to prove to you that they exist too. But also they insist on telling you where they've been: locations, locations. Everybody's little verbal guide-book to their lives. And Jonas would tell me all about his job, about how the next day he was going to journey all the way to Germany, and he would list the names of the motorways he would be travelling on, that he'd be taking the E30 through Poznan, the A10 around Berlin, and then he'd be on the A9, and past Leipzig he'd join the A93 along Eisenberg, Plauen, Hof, Cheb, Swiebodzin, Fürstenwalde, Weiden and Schwandorf until finally he reached Regensburg, his destination, at the confluence of the Donau, Naab and Regen rivers. How I enjoyed the monologues of Jonas Lutt!

Sometimes, I sat next to Mother in her post office counter on the wooden stool that Mother took there for its daily outing, licking the stamps for her, wearing aggressive looks for the benefit of the scaly Marta Stroud. Or I'd become a little lost wandering the city. I allowed myself to be upset by the growling of dogs chained up in yards, growls which instructed me to keep to my own part of the city. But slowly, slowly the city gave up its secrets to me, introducing me to tiny back streets which I had never known existed, revealing buildings which I must have passed countless times before but somehow had never seen. Entralla would sometimes sigh as I walked down a street and in its sigh it would introduce me to a balcony three stories up, brimming with extraordinary plants and pots or a small wooden house tucked between two brick ones or even a strangely shy mansion boasting two timid but muscly caryatids. When Entralla chooses to show itself, you must stop whatever it is that you are doing and allow the city to guide your eyes where it pleases, you must never continue on your journey saying to yourself that you will come back later, for when you do come back Entralla is sure to have withdrawn what it was earlier willing to reveal.

In those new days, I liked to sit on benches in Ventis Park and wearing skimpy outfits let the sun warm into every part of me, with human life all around, swirling about, being sometimes busy, sometimes not busy at all, just lolling about, loving to loll. But eventually, I'd wander the too familiar route back home again, considering that in the city I'm a timid thing, perhaps a few centimetres shorter than my real self, but at home, well, I'm at home. There, even with Irva and her inconsolable gloom, or perhaps because of it, I achieved full Alva height (186 centimetres).

And sometimes, when I was in Ventis Park, I might visit the zoo.

★　★　★

OPTIONAL EXCURSION 2. Entralla Zoo. *A third of our city's largest park, Ventis Park (trolley buses 7, 9, 14), is taken up with the City Zoo. If we lack human visitors from foreign countries we can at least boast animals from numerous foreign locations, but what sad faces they have, trudging dolefully around their limited homes. They can push their heads against bars and look across the way to see other animals, staring back at them from their cages, mirroring their own unhappy looks. Outside each of their cages are plastic signs with maps of the world on them, with a little patch of the world shaded red to indicate the region where each species originated. Elephants from Burma. Rhinos from Sumatra. Pigmy hippopotami from Liberia and Sierra Leone. Whale-headed storks from the swamps of East Africa. Giant anteaters from South Africa. Hamadryas baboons from Southern Arabia. Okapi from the Congo. Giraffes from the Sahara. Orang-utans from Southeast Asia. A solitary, retiring aye-aye from Madagascar. They are all here, all these and many more.*

What noises they should make: sounds from all the corners of the world. But these animals, for the most part, have grown silent, have forgotten themselves, with their food provided and with their enemies if not out of sight then at least cages away, they spend their days dozing in the shade, sometimes whisking away a fly or two that they imagine should be hovering somewhere about them, happy to ignore the children when they command them to come out of their huts to perform. Sometimes, it is possible to wander our zoo and barely see a single animal, and believe the zoo to be entirely deserted, but they are still there, the pot-bellied inhabitants are merely sleeping again, out of sight, dreaming perhaps of distant lands. So, to keep up the numbers of visitors, the zoo keepers – every hour or so – encourage the beasts out of their stupor by lobbing food over the bars, or by putting children on top of Mongolian wild asses or Arabian dromedaries, or by bathing the elephants with brooms and hoses while the public look on in amazement at those great animals sitting on their

huge backsides, resembling vast, naked old men with nose defects.
It was here that Alva came and, walking from cage to cage, longed
to break the locks, to set the animals free and to follow them all the
way to their distant homes.

★   ★   ★

Irva, so Grandfather and Mother had decided, was not quite ready for work, she should be left a while longer to recover, but I was given a post office uniform, and I wore it proudly. And this metamorphosis in blue fitted me like a perfectly tailored membrane, a second skin, as intricately mine as my own fingerprints. It was to be not only my profession but my personality. The post office uniform was a thing stronger than me, and it made me stronger, because the post office uniform was a thing of great certainty, it represented conviction and confidence. And as I wore it about the city, I became a part of the city. I was no longer timid as I went about my business, which was also – the wonderful truth of it – the city's business, now I was always at full Alva height. I was growing and blossoming. I was happy.

Two weeks before September broke I was already dressed every day in my post office uniform, proud of it, delighted by it, frequently seeking its reflection, terrified of dirtying it. Grandfather came to visit me, to inspect me, which was only right since I was part of his proud army now. But he did not come only to inspect me but also to bring me something. This object, my unceasing joy at it, had the insignia of the post horn thrice displayed upon it, and also upon its body were the words 'HI SPEED' and 'PRO-FRAME'. A bicycle!

'Let's see you on it,' said Grandfather, 'let's see you up and down Veber Street, let's see if you're really post office material.' The horror of it. The ignominy. The truth: I could not ride a bike. We are not born with the skill of bike-riding, none of us are, even those of us who will one day grow up to win that race of masochists, the Tour de France. Learning to ride a bike, once you have changed out of your post office uniform into something less sacred and once the saddle and the handle bars of the bicycle have been raised to their highest setting, contains the following ingredients: uncertainty, fear, perseverance, trust (in the teacher), betrayal (when the teacher first lets go of the bicycle), belief in the possibility of it, an intuitive understanding of the laws of gravity, desperation, exhilaration and plasters. Of course Grandfather knew I could not ride a bike. He had come to teach me. 'And don't suppose,' he said, 'I come calling on every one of my employees, don't suppose I taught all my workers how to ride. You are a very privileged young lady.' Indeed I was, I did not forget it. And I am very grateful to my grandfather for all the many things he taught me. But, to start with, I begged him, nearly tearful, not to let go of the bike as he trotted alongside me. Never to let go. And then he did. And after the third or fourth attempt, I understood that Grandfather was entirely right, it was all about letting go, letting go of fears and prejudices and shyness and allowing yourself the simple pleasure of breaking free, the joy of speed, the delight as the buildings lined up to rush past behind me. Look, look there: long girl on a bicycle, so high from the ground!

And I was off, and there was no stopping me, up and down Veber Street, and then out into Pilias Street, and then to the great beyond that was waiting there for me, leaving Irva behind as she looked down onto Veber Street from the attic window. And I could hear Grandfather calling out to me, 'You'll do.'

I, Alva Lina Dapps, took part in every form of written communication. If I was bad news one day delivering bills, then another day I might deposit a more happy missive, a letter of love perhaps. I kept things moving, I was one of the people who assured that we carried on being, I was all about movement. I posted, with absolute precision, pieces of outside inside. I was part of the great post office cog that helped to drive the vast machine of the city of Entralla.

I bought a padlock, I locked my bedroom, forbidding everyone entrance. Mother hated that lock; sometimes I would return from work to catch her sitting on Father's stool in front of my bedroom door, regarding the lock suspiciously, wondering why. And beyond the lock? The walls of my bedroom were decorated with pages pulled from atlases and with coloured photographs of architecture taken from a book titled *Famous Buildings of the World* and with other pictures taken from library books or saved from newspapers.

Sometimes I'd feel a sudden jolt of pain inside me as I worked around the city, delivering letters to my allotted portion of Entralla, and I knew that pain was because of Irva, and that pain I thought was the pain of us separating. She was barely my sister then, she had become something else, something that was built perhaps only of pain. When Mother or Grandfather demanded I spend more time with her, I'd leave the house. 'Go up and see your sister,' they'd say. When I refused they'd call it the cruellest neglect. I'd scoff, 'I never asked to have a sister, did I?'

But sometimes I would go and see her, sometimes I'd creep into her room at night. She always looked so pleased. I'd take hold of one of her hands, one of her bony and clammy hands, and press something into it, close the hand up again and leave. What did I press into her hands? Pieces of maps, shards of other lands. A torn section of Lurkistan in Iran, a ripped fraction of Flevoland from the Netherlands, a little paper gash of Beni from Bolivia. As a reminder that there were other places in the world, as a reminder that I would be leaving her. Sometimes I would open her mouth and place these crumbs of maps upon her tongue as if they were the body of Christ, and then close up her jaw and seal her nostrils and keep them sealed until she was forced to swallow. Sometimes I'd make her eat the whole of a continent in a single night. And since she never called out, since she didn't speak, I was quite safe. Sometimes I'd insist that she drank up an ocean, that she chewed, for example, the entire Pacific, popping it into her, nautical mile after nautical mile. 'Open up,' I'd say, 'open wide.' For months this went on, and that dumb doll that was my sister never complained. Perhaps, when it was all over, Irva had succeeded in digesting the world several times over.

Irva's skin seemed to me in those days thick with dust, and perhaps not just her skin, but all of her. A sister made of dust, dust face and skull, dust arms and legs, dust heart and lungs. If you blew on her then she would scatter into a thousand fragments. And she wanted to spread that dust onto me. And I wouldn't let her.

Every extra minute spent away from Veber Street seemed a kind of triumph to me. I longed to get out of the house and into the world. I would bicycle about the streets of the city, screaming out the names of other streets in contradiction, 'Regent Street, Broadway, Boulevard Saint Germain.' I'd revisit the library on People Street, coughing as I tore out the various pages that I could not bear to leave behind, pages which I might later force Irva to swallow, but after a time I was certain that the other readers in the library and the librarians were always watching me and I lost my nerve. Then I would spend my afternoons in travel agencies, leafing through brochures, marvelling at how wide the world was, imagining myself inside hotels, in front of castles, hiking through mountains. But the staff of those travel agencies quickly tired of me and, accusing me of dirtying and creasing their multicoloured destinations, would send me back out onto the street, barring me from the world. So then I began to revisit the Central Train Station, looking nostalgically up at the ceiling, seeing the trains as they arrived and departed, trains that had travelled beyond the borders of our country into other lands where different people lived different lives. I would watch those passengers arrive and depart with a silent envy. I would press my hands against train carriages, trying to learn from their touch the feeling of freedom. I would pick up train timetables and pin these to my bedroom walls also. I even once bought a train ticket and even stepped on a train, but the moment I sat down I began to sweat and tremble and had to clamber outside again, breathless and terrified. And what a look of resentment Irva gave me when I returned home that day. I wasn't able to leave. Not then. Not yet. I couldn't.

The padlock on my bedroom door refused Mother sleep. It disturbed her. Now as she journeyed to the post office every morning, she could see locks everywhere, locks to people's homes, locks to garages, locks to business premises. In the post office she regarded the numbered rows of boxes of those people that had their post delivered not to their home address but instead ordered it to wait for them in the post office hall itself. There's so much secrecy in the city, Mother thought, everybody's hiding something. Why can't it be like it is in the country, she thought, where she'd heard that locks don't exist, where people are accustomed to the far more sociable latch. The city was locking Mother out and she would not allow it. So one day she bought a hacksaw and went up the stairs to my bedroom. That evening, I came home to find Mother sitting outside our home on the entrance step. Miss Stott, I noticed, sat on her entrance step across the street, watching eagerly. 'I've been waiting for you,' Mother said. With tears in her eyes and matches in her hand, shaking the box in a very different way than Grandfather shook his matchstick boxes, she set light to my collection of photographs, some from books, some from newspapers and to my numerous train timetables, and to several tourist brochures and to sheaths of maps and whole countries from various atlases. And then our mother, burning the rubber soles of her slippers, did a little jig in the ashes. 'No one is going anywhere,' she said, 'families must stick together.' Mother rid the world of its maps, sending it in her efforts back to times before navigation – indeed, she would rather if Christopher Columbus, Vasco da Gama and James Cook had never been born, and if America, India and Australia had never been discovered; if they must exist, very well, let them exist, but not in her home. She would not have them there. It must be understood that in our Veber Street home the world beyond our city became as dark and unmapped as those many potential worlds beyond our galaxy.

In the future Mother always inspected my uniform and my room for maps every day; she searched through pockets, she lifted up carpets and mattresses; I was not allowed to enter the house without first being searched. In Mother's mind my maps were as poisonous to me as father's foreign stamp collection had been to him.

So then I'd store maps inside my post office locker. I spent more and more time in the locker room. I was not the only one there, some of the postmen liked to play cards in the locker room or to smoke or just to talk, and other postmen I noticed liked to store private things in their lockers too – for example, Postman Pirin kept his magazine of naked women in his locker, and in Postman Olt's locker I once briefly glimpsed women's clothing, tights and bras and panties and stuff all folded up. We yearn, we postmen and postwomen, we yearn, we yearn.

Often then, having finished my post office work, I would go to spend my money on food. I would sit down, always on my own, at some restaurant selling foreign cuisine, and, with my eyes closed, would set off on great imaginary journeys inspired by the taste of those strange platefuls. And as I sat in an Indian restaurant,[11] sweating from the dish in front of me, I opened my

---

11. INCIDENTALLY – *Gita's Indian Raja on Glass Street, tel. 316 32 47, still the only Indian restaurant in Entralla.*

eyes to see a framed poster of a young girl from that part of the world with henna tattoos upon her. That was it. That was what started it. And then, with discreet enquiries into the tattoo of a carrier pigeon on old Postman Coovin's right hand, I first heard of Pig Mikel.[12]

Pig Mikel was responsible for burrowing under the skin and depositing colours there with sharp needles for people who voluntarily subjected themselves to this torture and who even paid him for the privilege. He had illustrated his clients' bodies with samurai warriors, cherubs, serpents, Celtic bands, popular cartoon characters, wings, claws, motorbikes, naked women, numbers, skulls, Zen signs, swastikas, flowers, thunderbolts, any breed of birds, any breed of animals, a few Greek gods, personal messages of love and hate in five different languages, a thousand different names, fake scars oozing fake blood, and on one occasion a verse from the Bible, to be precise Leviticus 19:28, 'You shall not make any cuttings in your flesh or tattoo any marks upon you,' written onto the back of an alcoholic priest, who hooted with laughter throughout the process. Was there a thing in the world that he had not drawn on human skin? And there was scarcely a corner of the outside of a human being which he had not at some time or other been bent over, bothering with his needles. But Pig was not just a tattooist, he was also an expert at body-piercing. In his time I estimate he had punctured several thousand ears – some as many as fifteen times – several hundred noses, a good number of tongues, a fair quantity of nipples,

---

12. SPECIAL OFFER. *Mr Mikel has been pleased to announce that a reduction of 20 per cent will be awarded any foreign customers who appear in his shop carrying* Alva & Irva, the Twins who Saved a City. *He has even been so generous to add that the first foreign visitor to enter holding this book, will be given, entirely free of charge, but of course only if wished for, and wherever on the body requested, the following proclamation as a tattoo:* 'I ❤ ENTRALLA'.

numerous navels, a few lips, a collection of eyebrows, a score of foreskins, half a dozen slits at the tip of the glans penis and a vulva or two. And afterwards he always inserted a ring in these holes, and from those rings people jangled every type of object from the standard crucifix to the shrivelled hand of a chimpanzee – but that was their business, not Pig's.

Pig's person too was a great advertisement for his shop. His nose was pierced in the centre and a large silver ring hung down like a bull's, both his ears were thrice looped with thin bands of gold and his right nipple had a Celtic cross dangling from it, which he liked to fiddle with whilst he was thinking. On the top of his head, always thoroughly shaved, were two sentences in bold capitals flowing around his skull in a circle, so that it looked like the toque of some obscure holy order: the first, in the semi-circle facing the front of his head, said, I AM AN ARTIST; the second, to be read only when Pig had his back turned to you, unbashfully informed, I LOVE MYSELF. And in the centre of his forehead, in the same place that Rabbi Leow of Prague, Czech Republic, wrote on his famous golem, Pig had had inscribed the word 'PIG', which everyone called him because with his little eyes with their thick white eyelashes and his large upturned snout he resembled that beast, and was for some reason proud of the resemblance. I do not know what his real first name was, perhaps he was even christened Pig.

Into this man's world, one day, I arrived uninvited.

I stared at the decorations around the walls: a thousand photographs of different examples of tattoos. Often the customers entering Pig's domain would point at one of those designs and Pig would prepare his inks and his needle, take out a new pair of perfectly disinfected latex gloves from the box, the same gloves that surgeons wear, and let the torture begin. Often the client with his new disfigurement would say as the blood dried on his skin, 'Never again, never again.' But, or so Pig would have you believe, they often came back, for it was such sweet torture. 'Everyone likes the hurt,' he said, 'everyone needs a little pain, just to remind them that they're still alive.' But I had a different idea, I didn't want any one of those tattoos stuck up on Pig's walls, tattoos which perhaps several people had, I wanted an original design, and I was bursting to tell the tattooist what it was.

'What do you want?,' he asked, 'The Chinese symbol of strength on your ankle, or a daisy on your shoulder or a barcode on your arse?' 'I wanted, if it pleases you Mr Mikel, a map of the world.' 'Call me Pig,' he said pointing to his forehead. 'I think I've got a small globe design somewhere, where do you want it, not on your biceps, I suppose?' I took a deep breath and proclaimed, 'All over me, all over me. All over me. All over me. All over me. All. Over. Me.'

My instructions were neatly written out on post office paper. From the centre of me spreading east and west: Europe. Down my right side: the Americas. Down the left leg and waist: Africa. Curving round my right arm and taking up most of my back: Asia. Australia must take up much of my right buttock, and a proportion of the left.

Pig, incredulous, burst out laughing. I took out some money and pressed it into his hand. 'It'll take time,' he said, 'preparation.' I nodded. 'But can you stomach it? You'll feel like I'm tearing you to ribbons, you'll lose blood, your nerves will yell at you, and you'll have to be patient, you'll have to live with that pain day after day.' I nodded. 'And the seas,' he said, 'we'll have to squeeze them in here and there, cover all the rest of your skin with them, and what blue shall we make it – ultramarine, like in the Caribbean?' I nodded and smiled. 'Everyone,' he said, 'will want to swim in you. And your head,' he said, 'what'll that be – Scandinavia?' But then I said, 'No, you mustn't touch it, neither that, nor my arms beyond the wrists, I want to keep all of it hidden beneath my clothes, no one must suspect.'

'Once it's done you realise,' said Pig, 'it won't come off, it can't be undone, unless you want your whole body scarred.' I nodded.

'How old are you?' 'Nearly eighteen,' I said. Pig shrugged, sniffed, 'Payment in advance, shall we say, of each continent?' I nodded. Pig and I shook hands.

And so, a week later, the pain began.

Some people have been known to say that after two or three minutes the pain of tattooing goes and the skin just feels numb. Some people have been known to say that the pain of tattooing is a deep sexual pain that can induce orgasms. Some people have been known to say that the pain of tattooing is unbearable, a kind of blue pain that upsets the entire body, and, coupled with the sight of the tattooist's gloved hands wiping blood and ink away from the needle's path, can induce vomiting and severe mental stress. It is generally young people who subscribe to this pain, and those young people are often advised not to have the tattoo placed on a portion of their skin which will become, in time, wrinkled, so that as the beauty of the skin's elasticity fails, as our surfaces become corrugated and slack, that little piece of painted beauty on an ankle perhaps or a shoulder remains for ever taught, undistorted, immortal. Our teeth may fall out, our hair may desert us, our eyes may fail us, but our tattoos will go on, loyal even beyond the departure of our minds. So as aged and senile babies we may look at that strange person in the mirror who we are certain we have never seen before and wonder why on earth that person had chosen to have a phoenix drawn upon his chest.

Pig Mikel was a professional at his job, after all there are health risks with tattooing – inadequate hygiene can cause the spread of many types of viral infection. But Pig's needles were never less than sterile. It was with a certain pleasure that Pig viewed my half-naked nearly eighteen-year-old self, his blank canvas, goose pimples, small twin mounds of breasts and all, and it was with even greater pleasure that he advanced towards me, having made his preliminary sketches like those marks that hospital staff make with iodine, clutching the electronic tattooing implement, made in the United States of America. And so the loud whirring began. And with the whirring came the pain. So this was the pain. A heavy pain, not too sharp, at first seemingly bearable. But the pain didn't go away – the same pain stayed with me, neither lessening nor deepening; a pain that seemed to be slowly pulling off every millimetre of my skin. How my nerves twitched and sang and vibrated long after Pig's instruments had been cleaned and put away and I was far from Arsenal Street, back at home, examining myself in the bathroom mirror, behind a locked door.

As I clutched myself after those first hours of pain in our bathroom, I endlessly regarded and prodded the scab upon my chest, a scab exactly indicating the borders of our country. I must not pick at the scab, Pig told me, otherwise it would heal badly. And soon enough the dead blood flaked away and I was left with the map of our country that I had ordered, which selflessly took up only a tiny portion of my skin. And with what happiness did I rush to Arsenal Street, into the half light of Pig Mikel's parlour, and tugging off my shirt so that the pain could begin again, expounded, 'You can read the map of Alva!' Pig said, 'We can stop now, if you like. Do you really want to continue?' I said, 'Give me Europe!'

Some people write telephone numbers on the palms of their hands or upon their wrists, to remind themselves. I had the world inserted into my skin.

After our country was completed, mapped and coloured upon my chest, the rest of the world slowly followed. It made little difference whether it was India or Africa, Luxembourg or Madagascar, Saint Helena or Easter Island that were drawn upon me, blood and ink were shed in the same way, and swept aside by the gloved hands of Pig Mikel, in the same nonchalant fashion. Some days I would be at one with the pain and in a trance-like state calmly let it drill into me, some days it would beat me and I would clench my body and despite the protestations and insults hailed upon me by Pig would be unable to relax and on those days how the pain howled. Of course, there are certain parts of the body, in regard to this art of tattooing, that are more sensitive than others, the underside of the arms, for example, is particularly tender, or anywhere bony, particularly the collar bone, and so on the days when Alaska and Greenland were inserted into me or the central portions of Russia or Mongolia and China, I experienced a particularly keen agony and I left the parlour in a more dishevelled and miserable state than was customary, but I would return the next day just the same, eager for the horrors. I believed that it was only natural that the process should cause pain, how else could I get the grief and splendours, the historics, such histories, of so many different places to enter into me and stay with me always. The world was out there, but it was also, I thought touching my body, touching the ultramarine skin or the patches of me now coloured yellow or green or orange or red (the hypsometric tints of the globe), it was also here.

And all the while I was training myself to leave Irva. With each new country came the proclamation, the vow, the promise each time a little more strongly, each time with growing confidence that refused to be beaten, the sublime truth: Irva, I'm leaving you, every day I'm growing further and further away.

When Mother was asleep I would slip into my sister's room and removing my nightdress would show her the world as it was appearing. And Irva fretting, tears in her eyes, would touch those pieces of the world spreading over me like a blessing, those parts of me swollen in their newness. She'd moisten her fingers with a little of her spit and begin to scratch vigorously into me. 'No, Irva,' I said, moving her hands away, 'you'll need a knife to get it off, you'd have to peel me.' She kept shaking her head as if to say, 'No more, Alva, please, please, no more.' And always just before I replaced my nightdress I'd say, 'Look Irva, look how it's spreading.'

How well Pig knew my body, all of it, as he drew on me. I shaved myself completely for his tattooing, my arms, my legs, my pubic hair. Hairless for Pig. For so many hours he crouched over me as I lay hurting. But he never cared about the pain, and there was nothing about me that moved him; he admired my body only after he had left his marks on it. When he was tattooing Europe I could see the pores in his nostrils and the pits in his forehead, faces close up look so different. I tried to kiss him one evening but he only told me to put my clothes back on. When my backside had turned Antipodal he slapped it once in approval. And he kept putting the price up after each continent.

Then, finally, one day, Pig Mikel brushed away my blood for the last time. On that day he said, 'That's it, Map Girl, now you'll never get lost.'

Since I carried the entire world with me, what need had I for any further company? I was Africa and Asia, Europe and America, I was the seven seas, I was everywhere and all at once. Looking at me walking down Napoleon Street, wasn't it possible to tell by my gait just how important I was? Call it from our roof tops, pull all the bell ropes, whisper the news from person to person, 'The world itself has chosen to walk among our streets, our humble streets!' But the world was not on display, and so nobody quite registered the significance of this post office worker as she moved onwards, with untrusting looks, about her important business.

The world was hidden beneath my blue shirt (top button fastened), blue jumper, blue jacket and trousers, black scarf, black socks and shoes. The world was travelling incognito. But the weight of it was making me suffer. How could I keep such a huge and terrible secret, wouldn't I call out one night in my sleep and reveal all, wouldn't I mutter by mistake some day at the post office the words 'Pakistan' or 'Caspian Sea' or 'Canary Isles'? And wouldn't they immediately begin to ask me questions, such as, 'What was that you said, Alva?' An innocent enough beginning you may suppose, but what danger lay underneath it. What strange looks and whispers people would then begin to show me, what faces they would pull whenever I came near. Then their questions would grow brave and they would surely ask one day, 'Alva, it's so hot today, why don't you take off your scarf at least, we can see you're sweating under there.' Of course, I was sweating, I knew that. Wouldn't you be sweating if you were carrying the whole world on your person? But I'd keep my jacket on and my scarf and would hurry from the place. And then perhaps the questions would be put more carefully and cunningly, perhaps even these questions might become so brave that they grew into commands. Perhaps Grandfather would call me into his office one morning to say, 'Alva, you should be wearing your short-sleeved shirt at this time of the year, and even those short trousers which the post office has been so good to supply you with, I suggest you put them on and dispense with that winter clothing, the weather now being so summery.'

But how should I know which clothes to wear since I imagined certain parts of my body felt hot whilst others were cold? How could I possibly control my temperature when I imagined myself well below freezing at the northern end of my geomagnetic field (roughly 79° 13' North, 71° 16' West) commonly termed the North Pole, just below the nape of my neck, and I thought of myself as fading in the heat over an expanse of approximately 8,600,000 square kilometres of much of Northern Africa (let us name the space the Sahara desert), reduced cunningly, to half of the front portion of my left and my entire right thigh. So is it any wonder then that I, rather than wearing my winter clothing on the top half of my body and going almost naked on my lower half, chose to cover my entire self up, so that no one may know quite what limits of the scale created by that famous Swedish astronomer, Anders Celsius, I was pretending to reach beneath the covers whilst outside the temperature remained confoundedly, relatively constant. No, I kept the world to myself and to Irva. I spun myself around and around! And once I had taken all my clothes off it seemed to me, with only my feet below the ankles and my hands below the wrists and my head above the neck still visibly mine, that I was still clothed, only now my clothing was the world. I was unable to undress myself completely ever again. I took great care of the world, lubricating it carefully every evening with moisturising cream, just as Pig Mikel had told me to, though there was a spot around Lake Baikal (the small of my back) that hardly received any lubrication at all, but perhaps that scarcely mattered since the lake is the deepest continental body of water to be found anywhere on the globe. So what did I care about little, fiddly, human relationships when I was the whole world? What did I care? What did I care?

Some month and a half after I was living with the world, shortly after six o'clock one morning, there was another earth tremor. And this time there were casualties. This time a few houses lost more than their chimneys. This time a few walls sagged and groaned, and then buried twelve people. And when those twelve people were pulled out into the light once more only one of them still remembered how to breathe. There were cracks on build-ings, not terminal cracks, but warning cracks: step quietly, go to church and pray frequently. People began to walk in the middle of the roads now, viewing those buildings on either side with distrust and with fear. The shares of the scaffolding company of Mirin, Bao and Russell went up. The home insurance company of Collky and Platt feared bankruptcy. Parents let their children sleep in tents in Ventis Park. People played their stereos and hi-fis inside their homes at barely audible volumes. God became popular. The bishop applied to the Vatican to make Grand Duke Lubatkin a saint, so that he might protect the city. Pope John Paul II eventually politely declined.

It was the second earth tremor which made me finally understand. For who could argue with the vastness of a whole city shaking? How could a single person, no matter how tall, argue with that? As the city trembled, as buildings many times my size – so solid yesterday but now as frail and unconfident as old men – swayed in the tremor's wind, yes, as the surface moved, came the deep suspicion, the terrible worry, the suffocating thought that even though I was everywhere I would be going nowhere. The earthquake had made me realise that I was Alva. That I was only Alva. That was all. So there I was again, shrunken to the size of Alva Lina Dapps.

And these are the actions that surrounded my shrinking.

I was in my bedroom when the earthquake struck. Mother wrenched open the door to see if I was safe. I lay on my bed, my nightdress wrinkled up above my knees. Mother saw my tattoo. Mother saw a good portion of South Africa, and in that instant South Africa changed from being South Africa into an insult. And it was then that I shrank, I diminished in front of the slowly comprehending, and ever widening, face of Mother. Mother, mouth stretched, turned herself into a siren. She shrieked and screamed so much that Irva rushed herself into my room; she wailed so much and bellowed so loudly that some good people of Veber Street even came running, fearing some earthquake mischief. They pounded the front door open in their eagerness to enact neighbourly assistance, they clambered up the stairs in a crowd of altruism – the sound of which returned Irva immediately to her room before they had quite ascended – yes, they hurled themselves into my bedroom and it was only then, I suppose, it was only when they had halted, that they understood that the screams of Mother, which they had at first believed to be screams of distress, were in fact screams of vituperation. And they saw Mother, the siren, deafening with alarm, now about her daughter, pulling the nightdress from her, revealing, here and there, more bits and pieces of the world, for a second Australia was visible, until my determined hand forced the nightdress back down me and then perhaps it was time for Portugal to make a hurried appearance as Mother's thick digits went assessing the magnitude of the damage, or even a second of Canada or a flicker of India. And as the good people of Veber Street saw the whereabouts of these countries momentarily exposed, they began to understand that that tangle of arms and legs and shrieks and flinches was a jumble consisting of a distressed mother and a frightened daughter, and that such a thing was meant really only to be witnessed by the distressed mother and frightened daughter, and so they gradually began, all altruistic tendencies vanished, to descend the stairs of 27 Veber Street and even to collect themselves in a scrum of mutterings on the pavement in front of our house. And last to leave my bedroom was Miss Stott the tailor, who had entered our home empty-handed but was leaving it considerably burdened by yet another tale of Veber Street life which she would later whisper to her evolving suits and dresses.

Mother would be permanently ashamed now whenever she stepped out into Veber Street – which she did every day. She would never be able to shrug off that shame because as she walked hunched over down Veber Street it seemed to her that she could see a certain memory working inside the heads of all those neighbours of ours. And I too now avoided our neighbours, even Miss Stott, because I knew that they did not have the ability inside them to comprehend why it was that I had the world drawn into me. They could only see that there was something surely wrong, some deficiency in me which had caused such a thorough piece of self-abuse. And in their quick and fascinated and disapproving looks, and in the stories they afterwards told to those who hadn't been there, stories which were surely daily distorted, somehow the colours of my tattoo began to dirty; those blues and greens and yellows and oranges and browns seemed somehow soiled now, grimed by their exposure.

I was a girl who lived in a street in a city, tattooed and unhappy. From nowhere in particular. Going nowhere in particular. A young woman who, walking down certain streets of her city for the rest of her life, was certain to cause other people to point her out, 'There, that's the girl who has the whole world drawn on her.' Locally infamous.

Grandfather said, 'She's ruined herself.'
Mother wouldn't look at me unless I was fully clothed.
Irva came to visit.

Two nights after the tremor, Irva came to my bedroom to find me desperately scratching, feverishly trying to scrape the mocking tattoo from me, naked, but for the world, in agony and upset.

She took hold of me in her bony arms. She held tight. And in that grip, the strength of which shocked me, I could feel our hearts working stronger, beating in recognition. So fast. So strong. And I gave in, I gave in at once, of course I did, I gave in as soon as I felt the engine of Alva-irva stirring into life again, I gave in, I gave in, I couldn't stop myself. And Irva, a faith rising inside her, our reunion putting some little sound back into her, a piece of hope, whispered, barely audibly: 'My sister, the lonely planet.'

I belong to her, she belongs to me. That's just how it is, that's just how it is and there's nothing to be done about it. As if we were condemning ourselves to each other for ever.

The City in a House

The Plasticine City of Entralla

Gallery 25 of the Art Museum of Entralla, no. 1 Arsenal Street, is filled in the minds of many Entrallans with the Eighth Wonder of the World; others consider it, however, more modestly, merely a Spectacular Site of Entralla. Gallery 25 itself, taking up much of the third floor, directly beneath the great glass dome, is the largest room in the museum and was designed specifically to hold this

The Art Museum of Entralla

extraordinary work of art. It boasts a special climate carefully regulated to provide moisture and sufficient breeze to stop the miniature city drying out or gathering dust. The railings around the city's perimeter are to prevent the public from too much intimacy, but do take a visit to the upper gallery from which the city can be viewed from above in all its complicated totality, illuminated by the sky.

★　★　★

It could never be pretended, even for a moment, despite our reunion, that all was as it had been before the Central Train Station Adventure.

When I had drawn on my forehead, when the map had been written on my body, I'd so hurt Irva that she had sought a hiding place deep within herself. To find that place she had abandoned words and limited movement, until she reached an internal home so void of light, of such dank depression, so compact in its space, that she felt safe again. And now it was my task to carefully draw her out, in delicate stages, and with loving precision, lest she be permanently lost inside herself, lest I lose her and in doing so lose myself. I clung desperately to her, for she was, as I realised now, always and forever, my only company.

So time was all Irva again. Irva days and Irva nights, Irva hours and Irva minutes. I wouldn't leave her. I was her nurse, her constant nurse. I wouldn't allow Mother or Grandfather near, I pushed them away. I fed her, I brushed her hair, I washed her. She, in her turn, lubricated my map. We slept together in the same bed, in case she called out in the night.

So there we were, falling in love again.

Children say to each other that somewhere in the world there is someone who exactly resembles you, and if you ever see that person, your double, you'll fall down dead on the spot. But what happens if you were born with your double. What then? Alternatively, so Irva might say, I should consider how sad it was for all those other people, those countless twinless people, perpetually alone; who'll never really know what real togetherness is like. We were married, Irva and I. We even had a kind of marriage ceremony.

I measured the scar on my forehead and its exact position there. With a soft pencil I drew the mark in the precise sister location on Irva's forehead. I took out my school compass. While I held her heavy head steady, she did the deep scratching: the arrow, the 'N' for 'North'. Such eagerness, such passion in this new task of hers. Poor, tearful Mother couldn't understand. She never could. Some nights I unpicked Irva's scab for her.

When Irva and I were alone, and mostly we were alone, I would encourage her to trace her fingers across my map of the world. I would whisper to her, 'One day, Irva, perhaps we'll walk up Terminus Road into the train station and take the first train and go, just go and never look back.' 'But where will we go?', she whispered – and she only ever whispered. 'Anywhere,' I said to her, 'anywhere, right arm, left leg.' But we scarcely left the bedroom. Irva seemed to think that since I'd brought the whole world into Entralla, into Veber Street, that there was really no need for us to go anywhere else. Her voice may have returned but she was not yet ready to leave the house, she clung to her timidity.

I began to model for Irva plasticine buildings as gifts. To begin with that was all that she supposed they were, but in time she began to understand my great cunning. These buildings, Lubatkin's Fortress, the Central Post Office, Grandfather's house on Pult Street were given to Irva to remind her of what lay beyond 27 Veber Street. I was slowly trying to bring her back. Sometimes I'd even ask her to help me smooth out a wall or carve out windows or shape roofs. I said to Irva, 'Since you won't go out into the world, even out into Entralla, I'll bring it in here to you.' I'd win her back with plasticine buildings.

Some nights I'd catch her, tears in her eyes, gently touching those soft buildings, leaving her prints on their walls, or on other occasions looking out through the curtains into the Entrallan night, so close and yet so alien to her. She was trying so hard, her effort was such a painful thing to see, but she could not, she could not yet go outside, the very thought of it set her trembling again, sent her under the covers into her blackness. But she was, there could be no doubt about this, attempting to trick herself into trusting again. And she bravely began to build once more, to consider what it was that lay beyond our home.

I bought a cheap camera, I took photographs of Entralla streets so that Irva's miniatures could be more accurate.

After we had between thirty and forty plasticine buildings dotted around the attic, it all became clear. It was Irva who suggested it. We should build the whole city. I would bring it to her, building by building, street by street, the entire city of Entralla. With each new street safe in our home, how she'd recover, how she'd expand, how she'd slowly be encouraged outside once more. We would make a great detailed census. We would build a great plasticine model of the city of Entralla, not of a little section of it but of all of it, every street, every building. And we would find the nearest plasticine colour to each building, all those greys and browns and blues and whites and reds, all the parks would be of green plasticine, we would make a multicoloured Entralla, all the colours of Entralla! I would collect the information. Irva would build.

'And when it's finished,' Irva whispered, 'then I'll go out again, then I'll be ready, then I'll know what to expect. And perhaps, but you must be patient with me, perhaps we could even, and only after a time, and only perhaps, perhaps we could travel beyond Entralla, but only if we take Entralla with us, so we shan't be homesick. Yes, we must always have it with us. Yes, yes, this is it: Entralla in miniature in our trunks and suitcases. Yes. Yes.'

The plasticine city would be divided up into thirty-centimetre-by-thirty-centimetre squares. Each square a manageable size, small enough to fit within boxes or cases. Beneath each plasticine square would be a chipboard platform (thirty centimetres by thirty centimetres); I bought these chipboard squares ready-cut from the hardware store on Pilias Street. We were determined. Upstairs in the attic, the city began to grow, every day we saw it growing.

First of all Irva built Prospect Hill and then she crowned it with the Lubatkin Tower.

At the foot of the hill she began to build the cathedral. And as she built the plasticine replica, she tried to imagine just how it was for those ancient Entrallan builders. Each year they would have seen the cathedral growing higher and higher and perhaps wondered whether one day Heaven itself would be reached. Pinnacles, gables and flying buttresses. How long it took them, nearly two hundred years! (It took Irva nearly three weeks.) Sometimes as she sculpted the cathedral, in honour of the Holy Spirit, which smells of incense, I would light up a joss stick to help her into the mood. The cathedral is the single largest building in all Entralla, from it we would judge the scale of everything else.

After the cathedral's completion Irva's thoughts began to consist only of the old town. She was a Baroque and Renaissance Irva then.

The University of Entralla took up exactly six chipboard squares.

When she reached Terminus Street, she wouldn't build the Central Train Station, I had to do that.

On Sundays, Jonas Lutt used to come, he missed our chats together. He had been away from Entralla during the small quake, and the news of my tattoo, presumably passed on by some garrulous neighbour, seemed only to encourage his visits. He asked me to show him the tattoo, I politely refused. 'One day,' he said, 'one day you'll show me. Won't you, Alva?' I smiled. Irva decided she couldn't stand Jonas.

Jonas never stayed very long, he'd sit by the progressing city up in the attic and list numbers of motorways. Irva ignored him, she continued working away, those names meant nothing to her. On about the third Sunday, when I remember Jonas was wearing a T-shirt which said 'ANNE FRANKHUIS, AMSTERDAM', he announced, 'When visiting friends it is generally understood that you arrive with several bottles of beer or even a single bottle of wine, when visiting girlfriends it is generally understood that you arrive holding a bunch of delicately perfumed flowers, when you visit Alva and Irva Dapps it must be understood that you come bearing plasticine.' And then he held out a block of red plasticine, which Irva refused to build with.

Jonas never had any problems in telling us one from the other, he joked that I was the twin in colour, and that Irva was the twin in black and white, as if Irva's withdrawal from the world had included a withdrawal from colour.

Sometimes when Jonas came we wouldn't have time for his magnificent travelling stories, sometimes they'd upset Irva. She was frightened that I might be tempted away. On those occasions, Mother would make him tea or coffee and they'd sit together for hours in the kitchen, Mother patiently listening to Jonas's international lists.

Irva built the Financial District of Entralla, and the Television Tower, which immediately dominated the plasticine Entrallan skyline. From the top of the Television Tower, where there is a revolving restaurant that allows you to view all three hundred and sixty degrees of Entralla as you eat, and which I visited as I was making notes on the Financial District, I saw how far our model was from completion I muttered to myself and to all the vastness of the city, 'It is a truth: Entralla, whether of stone or plasticine, was not built in a day.' And still Irva seemed so far from ready to leave. She happily modelled buildings but did she really understand that these buildings actually existed just a little distance from where she was working away?

Now as I studied Entralla every day, as I saw Irva carefully modelling it, I felt I was understanding our city for the first time. The more Irva built the more I understood, the more it became our home. The city was reduced to combinations of spheres, oblongs, squares and cylinders, such limited choices. Irva was endlessly cutting these shapes, the angles of people's lives. Sometimes as she worked crouched over with her sharp knives and disobedient plasticine she'd prick her finger and a little blood would fall down onto a street.

With the buildings so reduced how much sympathy we had for the people of Entralla now. The smallness sometimes even made us cry: buildings no bigger than a fingernail; lives, then, smaller still. Irva cut out windows in plasticine walls, for without windows how could the people look in or out. She carved out doors too, all the doorways of Entralla. We feared for our city, the slightest jog of the trestle tables would set the buildings trembling, disturbing our hearts. We would often climb the attic stairs during the night to check that it was safe, we dreamt troubled nights of squashed buildings. We taped over the windows in the attic with black bin liners to stop dust and to keep out the sun which overheated our plasticine. We inspected the attic ceiling weekly, looking for hair-line cracks, we added braces to the tables' legs. Our profoundest instinct in those days: to protect.

Sometimes the old yearning would come back to me and with it, impatience. On those days I would cautiously visit the travel agencies again, always, during the city's lunch breaks, when the agencies were at their busiest. One afternoon I stole something from a display in an agency shop front. It fitted into my uniform pocket easily enough, I felt it belonged there, it seemed happy enough, and then I rushed out of the shop and ran whooping with delight through those so familiar streets. The object that I stole was a green plastic, fifteen-centimetre-tall souvenir of the Statue of Liberty.

And one night shortly afterwards, whilst Irva was sleeping, I climbed up the stairs into the attic, I placed the miniature statue, made in China, upon the plasticine city of Entralla. How wonderful it would have been if it were true, how wonderful to wake the city one morning and to see the expressions upon people's faces, as they rushed hurriedly to work and suddenly stopped short and with gaping mouths and wide eyes, saw that the Statue of Liberty had taken up home on our very own Cathedral Square.

That night in the attic, I suddenly turned around. There was Irva in tears.

Two large trestle tables held the weight of growing Entralla in the attic. There was a gap between these tables, to represent the River Nir. The Iron Bridge, the Senasis Bridge and the Small Bridge spanned these tables. On the model where the banks of the river ran, Irva attached small chipboard platforms to the trestle tables in imitation of the river's ancient path. If a plasticine man had inhabited the plasticine city and was in lonely despair, for he would have been the city's only inhabitant, and had tumbled from any of the bridges down onto the attic floor of 27 Veber Street, the fall would be greater than that experienced by the drop from the Grand Canyon in Arizona, America, and it is certain that he would be dead before his plasticine body dented out of shape on impact.

The model allowed Central Entralla to be seen with fresh eyes and to be seen clearly, for the first time, so comprehensible was it in its reduction. We could observe it from an impersonal distance now, as foreigners almost. Entralla had become strangely collectable. A thief might pass by and in a second pull out the bell tower from Cathedral Square and place it, lost to us for ever, in his deep pockets. The city belonged, now, in its limited size and dreams, to us, to Alva and Irva Dapps.

Central Entralla had been completed, we had reached up to and beyond the old fragments of Lubatkin's city wall, which, years before, when amateurs at this plasticine art, we first considered as schoolchildren. Irva had built the old town, she had built half of Napoleon Street, and still she was building onwards, onwards. But the trestle tables were full now and so we began to construct Entralla in fractions, chipboard square by chipboard square. When each chipboard square was completed we carefully lowered it into a box, of exactly the right dimensions, and then we placed a lid on that box, and we wrote on the lid exactly which fragment of Entralla was contained within. And the boxes began to stack up. All those boxes, which originally came from the post office, brown cardboard boxes that had once contained envelopes.

Soon it was time to seriously consider the sleeping arrangements of all Entralla, from the pavement to the humble bedsit all the way to the opulent town houses of Arkllitt Avenue. We began to give Entrallans plasticine homes to call their own, plasticine retreats to escape to, little plasticine corners of Entralla, microscopic crumbs of the world which were their microscopic crumbs and no one else's in which to express themselves, in which to be entirely, absolutely, unreservedly themselves; free from dilution of all other people.

From Grandfather, who was told so much of Entrallan life as he sat talking to his customers at the post office, we learnt news of three of our old school friends. Kersty Plint was pregnant. Eda Dapps had married Stepan Dinkin. We never asked for this news, we didn't want it, it got in the way. Irva stopped letting Grandfather in the attic. When he tried to build some of his matchstick locations in our home, the home of a plasticine city, Irva crushed them.

And then Grandfather stopped coming for a long while. 'It's as if they don't recognise me,' he said, 'and they stare at me, just stare, I can't bear them staring at me. As if they're growing wild. And Irva never talks to me, if she's something to say she tells Alva first and then Alva tells me. Something should be done, Dallia, it's not right.' 'Leave them alone,' Mother would say, 'they're fine with their plasticine. They only want to be left alone.'

Since I looked after Irva, and since I would not allow anyone else to look after her, Mother continued to work at the post office, and I began to work there only two or three days a week, as a part-time sorter. We had no room for Mother any more (the city was taking up so much space), and Mother at first tearfully and then calmly began to separate herself from us. I think it could be said that she was falling out of love with us then. We could feel her withdrawing, and as a punishment Irva no longer allowed her to see the city. She didn't seem to mind, at least, she never complained.

We didn't notice it at first, but after a time there could be no denying it: our mother, after twenty years, was growing independent and confident. She was letting go. She had her hair cut and dyed. She started dieting. She said to us in the kitchen one day, 'You mustn't forget your looks, because you have been caring for baby is not sufficient excuse, your husband won't appreciate a messy, sloppy wife. You should try letting him baby-sit whilst you spend a relaxing hour at the hairdressers. It will raise your morale a hundred fold and make you feel so good.'

Sometimes now, as a rest from my efforts, I would visit one of the cafés in Market Square. I usually went to Café Louis because Postman Kurt Laudus was often there, and he would always come over to talk to me. Sometimes I longed to speak to someone other than Irva. I'd sit at a table with a coffee and a croissant or a bagel or a baklava, still yearning a little, still yearning enough sometimes to lock myself in the bathroom to look at my map, and on those occasions, when Irva knocked on the door, I wouldn't always answer. In Café Louis I would gently chew those foreign morsels, close my eyes and relax. And whenever I visited Louis's I always felt guilty and in recompense I always brought back Irva's favourite for her, an Entralla bun.[13]

---

13. TREASURES OF ENTRALLA. The Entralla Bun. *Moulded to resemble roughly the shape of our most celebrated monument – the Lubatkin Tower (though I have seen some closer to the Eiffel Tower of Paris or the Pyramids of Giza or the Minaret of the Mosque of Samara) – the Entralla bun is a mound of baked dough, the crust of which is generally slightly burnt, coated in melted sugar. As a young boy, so our folk tale runs, when our city was little more than a collection of wooden huts, Lubatkin, aiding his mother in baking bread, dozed in front of the clay oven and when he finally pulled the bread out it was burnt and had formed an odd shape. That shape was the shape of the future fortress; from that moment on Lubatkin knew his destiny.*

All our plasticine buildings may not have been mathematically accurate, but they were, let there be no doubt about this, emotionally precise. And I should also explain that because Miss Stott once measured us so precisely with her tape measure, I began to understand that buildings could also be measured in this fashion. So often now – with a much longer tape measure than Miss Stott's, in a little metal box in which the tape coiled around itself – I would measure the widths of buildings and calculate the height by measuring the length of the ground to the first window and then multiplying it, because so often the different storeys of buildings were precise repetitions of each other. But mostly I just guessed, accurate guesses. (The fuss people made when they saw me measuring their homes, even if I didn't actually touch them. 'What are you doing?' they'd ask. 'Just measuring,' I'd say, 'I'll be done in a minute.' 'Why are you measuring my home?' they'd demand to know. 'Just because,' I'd say. 'But it's my home,' they'd all say, 'it's mine, how dare you!' 'Yes,' I'd say, 'I know that, but I want to measure it all the same.' 'But it isn't yours,' they'd say, 'it's mine, it's mine!' Is it any wonder that I often had to work late at night, when such hystericals were dreaming of thieves in their troubled sleep?) And of course I used our heights as a ruler also, I'd measure exactly how many Alvas or Irvas tall a building was.

Out of plasticine we built the ever growing cemeteries of Entralla, lines and lines of tiny squares, whole districts made up only of the dead, a whole city in itself. I never counted them all. There were simply too many little squares, just too many, too many dead people, too many living people. We couldn't fit everyone in.

Whilst making plasticine buildings it is important to warm the plasticine up first, to soften it. Before work, plasticine must be packed against the naked skin of hands, slowly warming it. If you are in a hurry it is advisable to roll two balls of plasticine and place one in each of your armpits. But never allow the plasticine to overheat for then it will stick stubbornly to your fingers, it will refuse to leave them, it will disallow any straight lines, it will refuse to be cut, it will mock you – buildings then will slouch and droop. You know that you have almost reached fluency in the pure language of plasticine when you begin to wonder, do I smell of plasticine or does plasticine smell of me?

Sometimes now, looking down on the plasticine city, to encourage Irva with thoughts of outside, I would read to her from the local newspapers. Together we would see, for example, where the robberies or murders had been happening, and if a robbery or murder had not occurred in the old town or in that part of Inner Entralla on the tables in the attic, I'd fetch the box holding the unfortunate street and we would stare suspiciously at the buildings, trying to seek out clues. But when I asked her to come out with me, just for a little while, just up Veber Street, as far as the bakery and back, she refused, she retreated into herself, wouldn't speak again for hours, and when she did, she yelled at me, 'You promised, you promised, you promised not until the city was finished. Don't break that promise now. Not after all this work. So stupid! I'm not ready yet. I'm not ready. I will be, I'm sure I will, I feel closer every day, but not yet, it's not time yet, the city's not finished, is it? Is it? So don't be cruel. I'll smash it, I'll crush it, see if I don't. We made a promise!' And so I wouldn't ask Irva outside again for several weeks. And yet every day she travelled in amongst the deep grooves of Entralla, her thoughts wandering through those many streets. She would set out on long walks, moving from box to box, studying from above the canals of streets, her confidence returning. She'd stroll round and around Entralla for hours every day and when she traced her thoughts back to Veber Street, when she closed the lid on the box of our street, it seemed to me she was a little out of breath.

There was another reason, besides our forced exclusion, for Mother's growing independence. Jonas Lutt. All this time Jonas Lutt continued to call on 27 Veber Street. He had long ago stopped bringing plasticine with him and he began instead to come with wine and flowers. If he ever happened to see either of us while he was at home, he always asked, 'How's the plasticine?,' and Mother would say, 'Oh, they just love their plasticine those two, they couldn't live without it, they just love it, go on then, you two, back to your work, Jonas and I would like some peace.' And wordless and appalled we would build on. And then one day Mother knocked on the attic hatch, she told us to come down, that she had something to show us. We almost yawned in anticipation but what she showed us surprised and shocked us. Mother had a passport! Soon Mother was going to go with Jonas Lutt in his Scania lorry all the way to Germany. Jonas had asked her, Mother told us with a smile, and she didn't feel it would be polite to decline.

We heard a great honking noise, we looked out of the window to discover Jonas Lutt there and his evil, stinking Scania lorry, and then Mother came out holding a suitcase, and she climbed into the lorry and Mother, for the first time ever, was going abroad. Mother was leaving us, in that monster of locomotion, disappearing up Veber Street, out into Pilias Street and away, away. And I was running after her until she was out of sight.

When Mother was gone Grandfather came to visit us again. We hadn't seen him for many months. When he saw Irva he said, 'This has got to stop, this has to stop. Neglect, that's what it is. Pure and simple neglect.' He tried to come close to her, I stood in his way. 'When did you last go outside, Irva? How long is it since you were last out? You can't stay locked up in here, it isn't right. It's not right.' We didn't answer of course. 'You're coming out now, you're coming out this minute.' He pushed past me and took Irva's hand, he was going to force her out. 'Don't touch her!' I warned, 'Don't touch her!' But Grandfather wouldn't listen, so I had to bite him, so I had to kick him and pull at his grey hair. And he was too old for us now and he couldn't beat us. He slipped down to the floor and when he was down there we both kicked him. He managed to scramble out of the house, his nose was bleeding slightly. I slammed the door. He sat on the doorstep for a while, I watched him through the keyhole, holding his handkerchief to his nose. Then he stood up, carefully brushed down his post office uniform and went away.

When Mother came back, only two days later, we pretended we hadn't missed her. She gave us identical T-shirts saying 'FRANKFURT AM MAIN' (Irva never wore hers), but she hadn't actually seen the city itself, only a depot on the outskirts. She showed me endless photographs of motorways, and foreign people in foreign motorway cafés.

In all the circles of Outer Entralla there were so many unremarkable streets, each seeming first cousin to the last, so much similarity that I sometimes found myself confused. And so now for the first time, just to make sure, I began to claim a little piece of every street or square in that place called Outer Entralla, so threatening in its vastness. I began to take a screwdriver with me always and as soon as I'd finished noting down or photographing a street, when no one was looking, I'd do my version of cocking legs to mark territory. I scratched onto the surface of brick or concrete at one end of the street, small autographs. I scraped: 'A & I'. It seemed only right since the plasticine buildings had Irva's fingerprints all over them, that I should mark them too.

How Irva missed me when I was away, how she sat at home waiting for my return. A life made up of anxious waiting. Each time I was gone she'd be unable to stop herself from imagining me dead, somewhere far from Veber Street, helpless Alva dead on a pavement.

Every day it took me longer and longer to reach new sites, every day I had to travel so far. But on I'd go, onwards and onwards, so that the city could be built. I was out so far, I hardly knew where I was, but still these distant streets were a part of

Entralla, still these people called themselves Entrallans. To think of all those Entrallans I had seen over the years! All those many Entrallans I had passed – the weight of seeing so many people, the endless busy numbers of them. The inertia they cause, how many little fragments of conversations I had heard, how many different shadows of words from behind doors and windows, how many times I had heard other people's telephones ringing inside other people's houses, how many times I had heard people fucking each other (for there are only a limited number of things humans can do together), how many condoms I had seen wrinkled in the streets, how many car alarms I had started as I walked Entralla, how many dirtied syringes with rusting needles I'd passed, how much I'd seen, the weight of collecting everyone, causing me such tiredness, such sadness.

And all the rooms of our home were filling up, from Central Entralla on the trestle tables in the attic to all the other boxes of streets and districts in every room in the house. All those boxes and boxes of Entralla! We were running out of space to put them, where could we fit them all? Where could they all be put? We worried more and more about space. The model had reached so far from Central Entralla that we had finally come upon the endless tall lines of the high-rise homes, cruel space upon cruel space. But where could we house these tower blocks of ours in 27 Veber Street? The spare bedroom, my old room, was completely full (on the bed, under the bed, around the bed), and even Mother's room was half filled with boxes of Outer Entralla (a whole half of the room cut off now by stacks of boxes) and some of the kitchen too, but we had been careful to leave a corridor between boxes, paths to the cooker, to Father's stool. And all those boxed were marked, 'DO NOT TOUCH'. 'DO NOT TOUCH' written all about the house. We had no choice, we had to pile them up, these towers, one on top of the other, and store them in their boxes in the cellar, out of sight, where we didn't have to look at them every day (just like the city planners).

And the city kept on changing, challenging us to keep up, old houses would be knocked down and new houses would be built on streets we had already completed. And so we would have to study that street again, add the new buildings. The city kept on changing, it wouldn't keep still.

In summer the greenflies and the mosquitoes and the house flies would come. They always knew where to find us. Mother would open the front door or leave windows open in the kitchen, and up they'd come. We'd watch them walk over our city, we'd see a hunched mosquito poised on some rooftop, we'd see a fat fly walking blackly, arrogantly down a boulevard. They'd swoop and hum around our ears, we'd long to crush them, we'd yearn to squash them against hard surfaces but we couldn't, we mustn't, we had to let them fly about us for fear, in our anger, some building, some precious square or even a humble plasticine pavement might be dented through our vengeance. We longed to kill them but we had to be patient, above all else we must keep patient. Can it be imagined how much patience is required to build a city? I bought fly papers. Our victims screamed and twitched on the sticky strips as we worked on beneath them, stopping occasionally to look up and smile.

But it was not only insects that we grew to fear. One winter came a new terror. When we were carefully checking through all the stacked boxes, as we happened to on irregular intervals, we came across one – of sector five including much of Bernadinn Street – which had a hole in its side. Something had eaten its way into the box, we could see scratch marks, teeth marks even. We placed the box on a table, and, trembling, lifted the lid. The horror of it! Poor Irva had to look away, had to sit down with her head between her legs immediately. The intruder had left its footprints all the way up Bernadinn Street; it had pressed its pestilential way deep into our carefully smoothed plasticine, it had casually pottered pitted footprints upon our work. But there was worse still: it had defecated along the streets, small lozenges of brown shit on our city! And worse of all, worse even than the shit, wrapped up in the corner of Bernadinn and Duvis Streets, at least where the corner had once been, for there was no remnant of it left, was the offending creature itself, curled up in a bed consisting of torn shreds of the persecuted box.

A mouse, if you please.

When woken, it fled through sector five, causing yet more damage, then leapt from the box and into the darkness.

We bought poison, we bought mousetraps. We raised our boxes from the ground using wooden boards and bricks, we carefully inspected them every day. We cheered when we found a hairy corpse, twisted on the floor. We felt no pity for its pain or for its tininess. Its length after all, including tail, equalled a quarter of many of our smaller streets.

Now that we had reached the furthest streets of Outer Entralla, Irva began to slow. As soon as I was out of the house she ceased modelling. She'd lie on her bed staring at the curtained window. Before, so much into her stride had she advanced with plasticine fashioning, it would have taken her a mere day to complete a complex building; now, with shaking hands, she hovered over plasticine blocks. She'd spend half a week on the simplest of structures. She knew that we were nearing the end and she was terrified of it. Sometimes, in practice, she'd allow me to place Father's stool in the hall passageway and she'd sit, looking at the door, sometimes she'd even walk up to it, but never close enough to touch. She'd look at maps of all Entralla and try to estimate precisely how much time she had left. The closer we came to finishing the more desperate she grew. To slow our progress still further she would secretly destroy buildings and blame it on the mice. She'd pick at random some innocent home and obliterate it with a scalpel, attempting with those tiny slicing marks to copy the claws of mice. If she was challenged, she denied it vehemently, she acted appalled that I even suspected her for a moment. She'd sulk, 'How could you think that, Alva, how could you?' She'd look at me, so sorrowfully, 'That you could even think such a thing.' And then for a while no mice, real or fictional, would approach the boxes until her terror at completion grew too much for her once more. She'd wake me up in the middle of the night. 'Listen,' she'd say, 'listen. Can you hear that? Sssh, you're being too noisy! Ach, it's stopped now. It was a mouse scraping away. There's a mouse between the walls. I'm certain of it. You would have heard it, you would have done if you hadn't made so much noise as you sat up.' But there never was any mouse there.

It is simply a fact that some people long to travel the entire world, and do not flinch from nights in wild forests or from the heat of the desert or from the anger of a tempest. It is simply a fact that some men long to climb the loftiest of mountains, others to explore the harshness of Antarctica, others still to circumnavigate the world in hot-air balloons. Why do they do it? For the challenge, we are expected to believe. And the newspapers and the journalists will not shut up about these people. But there are other, more modest people, whom for the most part the journalists avoid, who are frightened to step out into a street. It is a fact that it is too challenging for them. They cannot do it. This latter group of people, who almost always exist in solitude, are so panicked by the world that they close themselves up inside houses, inside rooms, and never leave again. The longer they stay inside the harder it is for them to peer out; they may be brave enough at first to touch door handles but very soon it will be impossible for them to turn them.

Sufficient plasticine construction has now been accomplished for me to arrive at a certain significant date: 15 July. To be precise, to arrive at the eve of Irva's excursion, on the day before she'd leave 27 Veber Street. On this day then, this unhappy day, heir to such misery, on this day perhaps six weeks before the plasticine city would have been completed, on this day, this day when I came home, predictably enough, from Outer Entralla, on this day, here goes then, on this day I found Mother had been cleaning the house in preparation for Jonas Lutt who was coming to supper.

Many of the boxes were in different places.

In different orders.

One had even been turned upside down.

She apologised of course, she kept on apologising. But we shrieked at her. And we opened the box which had been turned upside down and thrust the dented plasticine streets in front of Mother's face. And we crushed those dented buildings in front of her, pounded them with our fists in our exasperation, me strongly, Irva weakly, until Mother began weeping and even ran out of our house and up to Jonas's. And then a few hours later, after we had calmed a little and were slowly reordering our work, Jonas and Mother came in and Jonas started to tell us that we had been wrong to speak to Mother like that and we nearly turned savage with anger, and I said, 'Get him out, this is not his house, what's he doing in here?' And Jonas said we were being cruel and selfish. 'Cruel and selfish?' I said, and showed him the deformed and hunchbacked, misshapen plasticine streets of Entralla. But he didn't understand, he didn't understand at all. 'It's only plasticine,' he said. 'Wrong!' we yelled. And then I picked up Father's stool and asked Mother, 'What's this?' And she said, 'You know very well it's your father's stool, don't play games.' And then Irva pointed at Jonas and said, 'What's that? That's not our father, what's he doing in our home?' And Jonas said he'd come back later and Irva yelled, she actually yelled, 'Come back never!' Mother began to cry again, and then Jonas took her by the hand and out of the kitchen and even out of 27 Veber Street. 'Come on, Dallia,' he said, 'come home with me. You shouldn't stay here in this place, Dallia, with these creatures, come away.' Dallia? We thought for a moment, who was this Dallia? And then we remembered that Dallia was Mother's name. And then we wondered if she was to be called only Dallia now and never to be called Mother ever again. 'Come on Dallia,' Jonas had said, 'come home with me.' And then Mother, or Dallia, left. In fact, Mother, or

Dallia, slept the night at Jonas's. We waited for her, we sat in the attic all night with the hatch open, waiting for her return. We were still there waiting for her when the morning came.

Not so clever, Alva and Irva.

It wasn't anyone's fault, not really. Something extraordinary was beginning to happen, something had begun to fill everyone in Entralla with discomfort. When Mr Irt had told us in school that humans are insensitive to earthquakes we think now that he was telling lies. The day before, when the edginess was just beginning, I had witnessed Louis in his café in Market Square, smashing all his glasses and his cups, one after the other, hurling them onto the floor, and then pummelling the body and the face of Kurt Laudus. And from there, or so it seemed to me, the discomfort grew worse, it spread, multiplied, filled every street and home until everyone could feel it, but most people put it down to tiredness or nerves, or drinking too much coffee or the humid weather. But they were wrong, it was 15 July and no one realised then exactly what that meant. The animals knew though.

All round the city that early morning before Mother had moved the boxes, the hair on the body of every cat began to rise. Their backs arched and they started hissing. There was nothing that any human eye could see to make them so tense. But everywhere in Entralla domestic cats began to leave their homes. There were reports the next day that not a single cat could be found in the entire city.

In St Lekk's monastery on the outskirts of our city, in the monastery garden, lived five pigs. Happy, bloated, contented things. But on the morning of that 15 July the swine began to grunt and snort and squeal louder than ever before. The monks rushed out to discover why the beasts were so noisily disturbing their devotions, and when they returned with ashen faces the abbot was called for. The abbot was a gentle and sensible man not usually given to speculation, but what he saw that morning turned his stomach and his brains. What he saw he termed an omen of ill luck, a sign from above, a warning. The pigs had begun to eat each other.

On the evening of 15 July, while we yelled and screamed at our tearful mother, the animals in Ventis Park Zoo were panicking. The tigers were circling their cages, and leaping at the bars. The gorillas had taken hold of their cage walls and were trying to shake them apart. Monkeys moved with urgent rapidity, up and down, left and right, shrieking as if they were on fire. By nightfall even the most docile of creatures, the sloth, was active, shifting up and down its branches as quickly as its thick body would allow. The giraffes – usually such calm and graceful beasts – were sprinting, running at their tall cages, bruising and bloodying their chests. Lions roared, elephants trumpeted, sea lions honked, snakes spat, orang-utans thrashed, zebras whinnied, camels hissed; a swelling cacophony of misery was the zoo that night, with all the creatures in their own ways uttering the same frantic plea, 'Let us out. Let us out! LET US OUT!' They would not be calmed. The noises that night would have frightened the bravest of hardened soldiers; plug up your ears, run away, do not listen to those ugly sounds, for who could bear such unhappiness, it would break your heart. The keepers didn't know what to do, they could not open the cages and let the animals out, to shriek and charge down our city streets, so instead they fetched their rifles and loaded some with tranquilliser darts and some with real bullets. They put a lion to sleep, and a polar bear and a hysterical penguin, and they shot and killed one tiger who was scratching his mate apart.

And that will have to do for plasticine building for ever because, oh God, hold tight, here goes.

The World Loses Its Head

The World and Our City

The World, the third planet in outward distance from the Sun, is the only planet in the solar system known to contain conditions capable of sustaining life. The planet orbits the Sun at 29.8 km per second. It rotates completely on its axis once every 23 hours,

Entralla from Above

56 minutes and 4 seconds. Its lithosphere consists of roughly a dozen large plates and several smaller ones. Whilst moving about these plates can cause the phenomenon known as earthquakes. An earthquake is most obviously recognisable on the World's surface by a shaking of the ground. The city of Entralla, with the River Nir running through it, has prospered as a trading centre despite experiencing numerous earthquakes. Many historic buildings have survived, representing the Gothic, Renaissance, Baroque and classical styles of architecture. Manufacturing includes agricultural machinery, mining equipment, electronic calculators, clothing and foodstuffs. Population (estimate, before its most recent seismic activity) 475,100.

★   ★   ★

A beautiful summer morning, a few thin clouds in the sky, peaceful, calm, perhaps strangely still. The time was seven thirty-five. Clocks and watches all over the city were quietly and noisily marking time but many of them were about to stop and refuse to start ever again, no matter how carefully their insides were taken out and how lovingly put back together again. Time, a man-made device, was about to suffer a stroke. And time measured now seven forty-five. Nearly there. Hold onto your companions, take hold of something solid, a postbox perhaps, a street lamp, a building, but be warned, trust nothing, everything you had faith in before – put it aside.

It was seven forty-six on 16 July, a Friday morning. The inhabitants of our city were looking forward to the weekend, many were slumbering still and it might well turn out to be a slumber of a permanent nature. Some devout citizens were in the cathedral, the archbishop was reading his morning sermon, they looked a little bored, but they'd soon wake up.

It was seven forty-seven. And now came the quiet knocking, some of the people could hear that knocking, a strange sort of knocking that they had never heard before, it did not mean that there was anyone at the door, nothing so specific, their whole houses were being knocked upon, their whole beings, but so gently to begin with it was barely perceptible.

It was seven forty-seven and twelve seconds. There was no turning back now. Around the world in seismic stations scientists were about to report an earthquake measuring 7.5 on the scale named after the American physicist Charles Francis Richter.

It was seven forty-seven and twenty-nine seconds. After the knocking came a deep throbbing sound. The ground beneath began to rock slightly, first to the north, then to the south. The throbbing became louder. Then stopped. Then started again, deeper now, louder still. Then stopped. Then again, uglier, uglier. Rising, rising in volume until it became an inhuman snarl. Hands on ears. We were vibrating, we were being rocked like babies, except this mother had evil intentions. The earth, the earth was calling out, it was furious, it was screaming, it was in agony.

Everyone's china was tumbling into a thousand pieces, everyone's body was being jangled. Something was jangling all of us, shaking us violently, moving our bodies roughly into positions they had never known before. We couldn't stop it. Try as we might, we couldn't stop it. It had complete hold of us, we were its plaything. This was it, we all thought, this was the end, we were going to die.

And still we were dancing this unhappy dance, whilst about us the music of this dance, this monstrous snarl was rising. One continuous ugly noise. All over the city, everyone and everything joining in. It mattered little if people danced, people were always dancing but what if buildings danced, imagine that, and what if a whole city began to dance, imagine that. And the snarl reached its ghastly climax. And then? Silence.

That was how it felt. But how did it look? On St Lekk's Hill, overlooking Entralla, one man reported that he could actually see the city sway like a field of corn in the wind. But buildings don't sway, buildings are supposed to keep still, that's what we like about them. Buildings don't like to sway, it upsets them, they go on strike, they revolt, they give up. From his advantageous position the witness saw that the buildings were indeed beginning to give up, but he saw it only for a second because then a vast cloud of dust began to rise and with it the witness immediately lost his usefulness.

In the city that fateful morning it was no benign cloud that had risen but a hurricane of stone dust which howled about the toppling streets, it blocked out the sun, turned our city to night, darker, darker than any night, it shrieked in and out of the broken windows of the thousands of now disintegrating rooms, it blew people against walls and out of buildings, it was a shriek and a howl in direct competition with the snarl of the earth, and within it, like the sounding of a triangle barely heard in a swelling concert, glass cracked, steel snapped, whole buildings groaned, but there was not a single human sound. Not yet.

The city, too excited by this metamorphosis, began to get carried away, in the epicentre of the quake, reckoned to have been on People Street, it behaved with particular cruelty towards its structures. The whole street was lacerated, its buildings flung this way and that, pavements rose four metres, houses sunk until they could no longer be seen, gas pipes were ripped open, electricity lines torn away from their poles and in desperate spasms flung themselves everywhere, whipping the shattered street and its shattered buildings, starting fires. Now in fear the bells of all our churches began to toll, clanged by some unseen, petrified hand, as if our city was opening its throat and calling out for help.

So many people of Entralla that morning felt the earth give way beneath them, or saw through rhombus windows, in the dimness, that the houses across the way were being played with as if they were paper places. They were being torn into little balls and hurled along streets for kilometres and finally deposited, as if suddenly the game had been abandoned, at an entirely different address.

The world, the whole world, the people of Entralla would have you believe, and they were convincing enough, was at an end. And who could doubt them, for just then in our old school on Littsen Street the geography classroom on the second floor tumbled to the ground, shattering in the playground, and for a moment the sky was filled with pages of textbooks and children's essays, from the excellent to the appalling, peacefully floating downwards, essays on every country in the world. And the several globes of that classroom broke free from their stands and began to roll hurriedly down Littsen Street, free at last, until they finally stopped at the bottom of the street, no longer legible and misshapen now with dents and with an ashy grey colour covering them as if the earth had become the moon.

Tall buildings could be seen fainting onto smaller buildings who could not or would not carry their weight. A grandmother on the ground floor of a house on Wilm Lintel Road saw her two grandchildren, one a boy, one a girl, smile at her in a strange way quite out of keeping with their age, and then an instant later, after her home had let out a single brief cry, and once the dust had cleared, she saw that her grandchildren had been replaced with her entire bathroom and that her bath tub and basin had taken their places.

On Trinity Square, on the outskirts of Entralla, tall residential blocks, each fifteen storeys tall, collapsed into massive corpses, into piles of rubble of inconceivable largeness. People's homes concertina-ed from fifteen floors into seven or even five. One block at the eastern end of the square was cut in half, so that half lay in jagged heaps on the square floor, while the other half remained standing. This bisected residence was reminiscent of dolls' houses that open down the centre, revealing the rooms and their contents in two equal halves. In that remaining portion of a block, half a bedroom could be seen with half a bed, half a bathroom with a bath but no lavatory, half a sitting room with shelves and a television but no chairs to sit and watch it with, half kitchens with cookers but no refrigerators. Half apartments stretching all fifteen stories upwards, with only half families left inside them. Lovers had held hands as they lay asleep in their bed, the female on the left, the male on the right, but when the female awoke her hand was empty. If she moved over in her half-wakefulness hoping to find his warm body she too would have tumbled all the way down onto the broken floor of Trinity Square.

In Cathedral Square, on that particular morning the cathedral bell tower was ringing its bells excitedly as the cathedral began swaying dangerously from left to right and the great roof began to collapse. Earthquakes are unfathomable things, they will obliterate one building, yet leave its neighbour a little dizzy but otherwise unscathed. Above the cathedral, on top of Prospect Hill, Lubatkin's Tower, seemingly indestructible, stood firm, for some keeping hope alive; for as long as the tower still stands, so long do we have a city called Entralla. And as the cathedral at the foot of Prospect Hill lost interest in all the statues in its niches and let them shatter in the square, as its pinnacles snapped in two, as it spat its masonry ornamentation away, as portions of its roof tumbled down slapping the floor of the nave, Lubatkin's Tower was kept company by the bell tower which only wobbled a little, in sympathy perhaps. Within the cathedral itself the appalled archbishop looked out from his pulpit from which only moments before he had been delivering his sermon; as the dust cleared a little he saw rubble in front of him and a few dishevelled and dusty parishioners, rag dolls dispersed about his church.

Constantin Brack, our celebrated sculptor, in his studio on Jay Street, just beginning his work, saw various full-length marble people dancing across the floor towards him, never changing their expressions once. He opened his arms to receive them and they crowded in and crushed him to death.

Our mayor at that time, Rinas Holt, sitting at his breakfast table in the mayor's residence, saw the heavy metal crest of our country lift up from the wall and strike him rudely on the head, spilling his brains into his bowl of cornflakes and turning the milk pink. What a time to lose a mayor, who would look after us now, now that we needed looking after more than ever? Ambras Cetts. Ambras Cetts was the man. Ambras Cetts had been spending the many years of our plasticine building climbing up the political ladder until, as the earthquake struck, he was assistant to the mayor of Entralla. Ambras Cetts, yes, he was the man for the job.

Now it is time to consider a map, and, for the sake of familiarity, the map I wish to consider is the map on the wall of Grandfather's office. I imagine that map of Grandfather's shaking now also, I imagine it fluttering in the earthquake's foul breath. And I see, with closed eyes, that as the map thrashes against its drawing pins that Grandfather's office is going berserk, throwing stamps and envelopes and Grandfather everywhere. And now the electricity cables commence to caper about, sending sparks flying, sparks that even strike Grandfather's defaced map and even Grandfather himself, igniting his formerly impeccable uniform. I imagine the map ripping apart now, I imagine the heat of those sparks setting fire to parts of the city, whole streets are in flames. Fragments of paper, fragments of a people, fragments which contained so many lives are floating to the ground now, and when these shards hit the ground about the real city they make noise.

And what of the people who were inside the now burning Central Post Office that morning, with its twelve wooden counters which ignited so easily, what of them, these panicking post office workers, among them an elderly postmaster and a postwoman with a mole on her cheek, yes, what of them, with the main entrance door of the post office still locked, since it was several minutes before opening time, and so blocking off their main exit route, yes, yes, what of them? What of them? But concentrate, concentrate, I tell myself, it's maps I'm talking of now, not people. So I leave the map in the Central Post Office, for it has become illegible, and take another. I remember, because I could never forget it, a certain three-dimensional plasticine map once situated all over the rooms of a Veber Street house.

The plasticine city was shaking too. And as the model shook, it began to spill buildings. The plasticine city was alive! Whole streets now were lifting off the trestle tables, mixing themselves up with other streets as if someone were trying to redesign our city, and as these places leapt from their ordered destinations some casualties were inevitable. Buildings fell to the floor, but once there, though now in strange bent and twisted shapes, would not be content but continued to dance still further and further away from the mass of our still jolting and jerking city, as if they were no longer satisfied with belonging to our city at all and had started journeying towards other distant cities that they believed might suit themselves a little better.

Consider Entralla now: Napoleon Street, the Paulus Boulevard, People Street, simply jiggling to their death. What a sight, unbearable even, or perhaps especially, when acted out by plasticine substitutes. Imagine it for a while, falling apart and then, after three or four minutes, and quite suddenly, the city was still once more.

All I have said so far is part of the much bigger story of Entralla and its quake, but now I wish to talk not only about our city but also to show how little, commonplace people fit into the large sweep of history. History is not all mayors and sculptors and catastrophes. Sometimes it is long-distance lorry drivers called Jonas Lutt, and sometimes it is even twin sisters as well.

In Veber Street, in 27 Veber Street, in the attic that morning, Irva and I lay on the floor with plasticine buildings all about us. Our long legs bent at unaccustomed angles, Irva's dress rumpled high about her waist, as if the earthquake had been trying to get inside her.

I wondered if somehow I had leant too hard onto one of the trestle tables and in so doing had set the city rushing away from itself. But then I thought, how was it that we were both on the floor? There was a portion of Entralla University on my lap – I briefly considered that it might be seeking comfort there. I saw two buildings from Pulvin Street leap from the table, bumpily cross the attic floor, hover over the edge of the open hatch and then disappear into the passageway below. And then I heard a great crashing. Surely, I thought, surely those two plasticine buildings from Pulvin Street tumbling down onto the landing would not make such a sound. Then I considered that the crashing must surely have come from way below, from down there in the kitchen, all that way away. I'll have to go into the kitchen, I thought, I'll have to travel all the way into the kitchen to see what it was that crashed. Perhaps Mother's come back. But then I heard another crashing which sounded as if it was coming from outside, all the way outside, past the front door and beyond the doorstep. I began to think then that perhaps it wasn't only the attic that had been affected, or even only our hallway, or kitchen, or even only our house, perhaps, I thought, my thoughts stretching to allow several houses in now, perhaps Veber Street was affected also. And then I very slowly heaved myself up and I saw the piece of Entralla University equally slowly collapse onto the floor, in a converse motion, and I gradually journeyed towards the window, moving with such unnatural slowness, as if I were one of those foreign men who, on occasions, are sent up into space. And as I trudged towards the window I stepped upon a building by mistake. It was, I think, I can't be sure, a building from Market Square. I squashed it quite completely. And then I pulled away the bin liner that covered the window and looked out through shattered glass.

Sometime between the end of the noise of the buildings and the commencement of the noise of the people there was a silence. All clocks were stopped. Time too needed a little rest. People now were getting up over so many different floors considering this: it's stopped, it's over, we've somehow made it through. But they could not speak. Not quite yet. Many others tried to call out but no sound came, it was too soon, there had to be a silence. Around the city, dust clouds began to thin a little. Peace, peace, it's over.

Now everyone could move under their own will, nothing else commanded them, they were learning how to use their arms, their legs, their heads all over again. But they moved with heavy, unhurried gestures as if in slow motion. They were not yet able to comprehend what it was that had just been done to them, why their homes no longer resembled their homes, why their entire world had been turned upside down. How long did the silence last? A second? Ten minutes? More? I cannot say exactly, it's impossible to really say, and some people found that this silence was for them a continuous silence.

Then, finally, perhaps under the struggling determination of the minute hand on the miraculously still functioning clock of the City Hall, a measurement was possible. That minute hand moved from seven forty-nine to seven fifty, and beneath it there was a mounting rush of wind that was really the wind of sound being put back inside us. And immediately we found ourselves moving at more natural speeds and we opened our mouths to call out, some people called out for help, others called out people's names, others still called out in frustration at buildings, buildings that had moved, without permission, to places they shouldn't be, or they called out in blame, in rabid blame because a building, which looked as if it belonged in Market Square, had been mistakenly stepped upon, had been defeated by a foot.

'A building! A whole building!' As my sister screamed at me for my carelessness, I turned round to her and said: 'Irva, it was an earthquake, there's been an earthquake.' 'I don't care,' she said, 'look what you've done.'

'Irva, we have to get out.' 'A whole building ruined! Hours of work! Such clumsiness!' 'We have to go outside.' 'Fix it now!' 'We must go out now.' 'What are you talking of? Get to work!' 'Listen, Irva, there's been an earthquake. We have to get out.' 'I don't go outside, Alva, you know that.' 'But that doesn't count any more, don't you understand?' 'We made a promise.' 'Come out with me, it'll be all right.' 'No, Alva. Draw the curtain and we'll forget all about it, even about that building you stamped on.' 'Out you come.' 'Seal up the window!' 'Give me your hand.' 'I will not.' 'Give me your hand, Irva.' 'I can't. I can't, Alva. Stop it now. Stop it and get back to work!' 'Your hand, Irva, your hand!' 'Never, never, never, never, never, never!'

And then we heard our home humming to itself and then wheezing and then moaning in its unhappiness. And then there were snaps about us, strange shrieks of wood.

'Irva, quick now, don't fuss.' 'I can't. I CAN'T!' 'You can, Irva, you will.' 'THERE IS NO OUTSIDE!' 'Come on, girl, come on now.' 'My heart!' 'Out, Irva, now!' 'OUT?' 'That's it. Come on.' 'OUT!' 'Good girl, that's my Irva.' 'Out and leave the city? What are you saying? I can't leave the city! Who will look after it?'

And then I was pulling her, tugging her, pushing her, dragging her away from the city, out of our home, into Veber Street.

Indeed, earthquakes are unfathomable phenomena and in them, and falling out of them, odd things happen. Earthquakes lose so many objects, everyone knows that, but also, they find many objects too. For example, whole chunks of the ancient wall that used to surround Lubatkin's city burst out of newer buildings, destroying them in the process. For example, within the cracked playground of the school on Littsen Street, time capsules deposited there by so many generations of school children were beginning to peak out now. For example, people who have disappeared for many years suddenly turn up again.

The door of 27 Veber Street was pushed, heaved open because it had suddenly become so stiff, and standing there on our doorstep were pink Alva and pale Irva.

Outside again.

Under the naked sky.

And Irva said, looking about her, holding onto me with both

hands, confused and offended and terrified: 'This is not Entralla! This place – where is it?'

Nothing was familiar to her. She had no idea where she was.

During the construction of the plasticine city, Irva had slowly begun to trust again. She believed in all those plasticine streets, they represented a certainty, a profound truth, she could imagine herself walking down them, she could make no sense of the affront she saw before her now. She frowned at what she saw. Her nose wrinkled up. Her eyes, adjusting to larger objects than she had seen in so long, hurt her.

If the plasticine city did not represent what was outside our home, if that too lied to her, then what could she trust? And, worst of all: where could she live now?

What Irva saw that morning was of course, once upon a time, Veber Street. And who could blame her for her confusion, for where had Miss Stott's tailor shop gone? And wherever it had gone, had it taken Miss Stott and all those stories and dresses and suits away with it? And what had happened to the baker's and why was the butcher's shop missing its front?

Now Veber Street began to fill with other people, slow, slow people. And with such people as we had never seen before. Were these truly the inhabitants of Veber Street? How different they looked, these half dressed and dishevelled ones, who stumbled about, limping into the centre of the street, huddling around each other. Deathly quiet. What a variety of strange possessions they were holding. As the earthquake struck, as people left their homes, they took with them whatever was nearest. One old woman held her chamber pot; one girl a hot water bottle (cold now); one man a canister of shaving foam; another a bottle of vitamin tablets; another a box of eggs. As if these objects were the most precious things in the world to them. These were our people of Veber Street, look what had happened to our people of Veber Street, look what had been done to them, all dressed in the same uniform grey, grey from the exhalations of crumbling buildings, grey skin and hair, unhappy faces peering out through the misty light. And this was the worst of it: they all had the same expression. Every single person of Veber Street looked the same, as if they had all come from the same womb. They looked hurt. Not with physical pain. But offended. Their sensitivity badly stung. They looked betrayed, like Irva, as if something or someone they trusted had cruelly wronged them. Slowly, slowly the people of Veber Street were able to understand what had happened. If not by sight, then by smell. They could smell the scent of freshly bled buildings, brick dust, smoke. They began to look about them and saw people lying silently in the tipped street. They should've got up by now, they thought, if they were going to. How their stillness was resented. Stilled people in our street hanging out of half dead buildings, people in our street flopped over walls, their shirts and skirts gently moved by the wind. But sometimes it wasn't whole stilled people whom they saw in our street, sometimes it was little bits of people, often not recognisable as the bits of people until they looked harder: a hand peeping out of rubble, with an eternity ring still on its finger, or a buried leg with a perfectly usable shoe at its end. And they saw, standing on the doorstep at one end of this street of ours, this street which we have lived in for so long, this street which is our home in the world, they saw twin women. One of them in a post office uniform, the other in a dress with long greasy hair and a face so white it looked as if it had been painted on. Strange, they thought on this strangest of days, we had only seen one twin for such a long time now that we presumed the other one must have died.

Now from our doorstep vantage point we saw someone we instantly recognised: Jonas Lutt. The presence of Jonas Lutt was yet another reminder that earthquakes certainly do not only concern sculptors and mayors, collapsing apartment blocks and female twins, sometimes they are even about our street, and sometimes they are even about long-distance lorry drivers.

Irva looked at me briefly in terror, and rushed back inside our dying home.

Jonas Lutt, in 12 Veber Street, alone in his bedroom – which our own mother had recently quietly tip-toed away from that morning to journey to her work at the Central Post Office – had been woken by the earthquake. His initial earthquake experience was not one of horror but of mild amusement. He was woken by a terrific banging. As he opened his eyes, he saw that somehow his chest of drawers was alive. Jonas watched it as the quake bounced him up and down naked upon his bed. The chest of drawers, which was a Lutt family heirloom and was an expensive piece of genuine Rococo furniture, originating in France, and built in the year 1720 (approximately), moved around the bedroom, turning on itself, spinning on a single corner, bowing to Jonas, its drawers moving in and out as if some invisible force were desperately searching for a piece of its clothing, slamming the drawers shut, and then pulling them open again. Just as the thing decided to march straight towards him, the rumbling halted and, as if suddenly shocked, it collapsed, falling with a crash onto its back, its little legs quite still again.[14]

As Jonas leapt out of bed he noticed that great gashes had appeared on his bedroom walls and as he stood at his window he heard the crashing begin all about the city. And then in a panic

---

14. LOST TREASURES OF ENTRALLA. The Chest of Drawers of Jonas Lutt. *Jonas Lutt looked suspiciously at that chest of drawers so many times in the years following the earthquake, waiting for the malignant force to set it moving again, as if the fate of the city could be determined by the activity of a single bedroom object. Sometimes, waking after bad dreams, he would lurch for the bedside light to check whether the chest had begun to live again. It watched him sleeping on so many nights with an attitude quite out of keeping with objects*

he remembered our mother and called out our mother's name, 'Dallia, Dallia!'

And I watched him that morning, briefly, from our doorstep, charge up the place that used to be called Veber Street, and then I looked away and hurried inside our home after Irva.

Our home mumbled and whined but still, for the moment, kept upright. Irva was inside, in the listing attic, by the city, returning the buildings to their correct places, trying to make everything right again.

The city of Entralla was missing a few of its key monuments, and certainly in many places it had been jumbled about, but it was mostly still there, still noticeably its triumphant self, still an undoubted miracle: our plasticine city. And Irva would not leave it. She turned her back to me and continued her work. No. 27 Veber Street muttered and sang to her, as it foundered. She wouldn't come out, we'd made a promise, she kept repeating, she couldn't leave the city, who'd look after it if she didn't. I tried to force her out, but she kicked now and bit and wouldn't be persuaded. I explained the terrible danger, but all she would consider was her plasticine city, which she could not, she implored, could not abandon.

I ran back out into Veber Street, I begged our neighbours to help, to drag my sister from our home, but they looked away. 'She's all right,' they said, they had seen her just a moment ago. They were more concerned with people they hadn't seen since the night before. 'Don't bother us now.'

---

of domestic usage. About ten years after the earthquake, he woke up once again to stare at the chest but this time he had had enough. He heaved the thing out of the bedroom and into the passage. The next morning he pulled out its drawers. He took it drawer by drawer and then finally its empty cage, into the street and dismantled it with an axe, happily chopping the thing to splinters. And then he burnt it. And as he burnt it he considered that he was by this act ridding Entralla of any future calamities.

What could I do? I looked around, asked more people for help, I begged them, but they ignored me, or pushed me away. I saw people carrying their expensive objects out into the street, I saw an old woman heaving a grandfather clock as if it were her fainted husband, tall and stiff. And suddenly, in that moment, I realised that there was only one way that I could bring Irva out, one certain way.

I went back inside. I took hold of one of the boxes, I brought it out. I took hold of a second, a third, a fourth. Irva called out, 'What are you doing? Where are you taking them? Bring them back!' Slowly, box by box, each box containing its plasticine jewels, I brought Entralla out onto the street and carefully stacked it as I heard our house chatting away to itself, sometimes gently, sometimes not.

After a while, panicking, as I moved now with five or six boxes at a time, she tried to work out where there were more boxes, in the house or in the street – her loyalty divided now, her love challenged. She was being forced to abandon at least a part of the city, she was being ripped in half. And she never once dared to take a box from me. I had it in my hands, she was too terrified for the contents, she loved them too much. Where should she go, in or out? Out or in, Irva, which is it to be? 'Please, please stop, I beg you!' But out it went box by box.

Barely half an hour after the earthquake had struck I set about saving the city.

It took Jonas Lutt nearly three hours to reach Napoleon Street, the roads had become so confused and misleading and sometimes had completely disappeared. He ignored all the calls for help he heard on his way, he was too busy, he hadn't time to stop, and to those in distress he answered cordially: 'I'm sorry, I'm in a rush, later maybe, not now, sorry, sorry.' Outside the Paulus Hotel on the Paulus Boulevard he saw guests dressed in every conceivable fashion of nightwear, such colourful displays of candy stripes and paisley patterns, floral designs and silk slips, quite unsuitable for the occasion. And as those guests swapped their stories, they looked across to the other side of the street and became suddenly quiet. Half of the Paulus Boulevard had been reduced to steaming rubble. But on Jonas marched and as he marched onwards he passed many other people travelling in the opposite direction surely on hurried missions not dissimilar to his own on this day of a thousand, thousand tragedies. He felt that he might be too late, he felt that something terrible had happened, he thought that he might have lost her, but he prayed he was wrong. Let her be all right, he prayed, let her be all right, God in Heaven let her be all right. But God in his heaven had other things on his mind, as Jonas Lutt finally turned into Napoleon Street.

There were nearly eight hundred individual boxes in Veber Street, all neatly stacked up, all calm and saved. And then in I went again. Careful, careful. Irva was sitting on the attic floor, holding onto one of the table legs. Shivering and speechless. I took up the chipboard squares that supported Prospect Hill, I pulled Prospect Hill from the table, Lubatkin's Tower shaking slightly. Irva looked at me, exhausted, defeated. She let go of the table then, she followed me, a few steps behind, out of the house into Veber Street. And there she stood, in the street. Finally. Irva. Outside.

I gave her Prospect Hill. She nodded. She held onto it. And she waited there in the street for me with the hill and the fortress in her hands, calmer now, with the boxed city all about her. I went back inside to rescue Central Entralla.

When Jonas Lutt reached Napoleon Street, stumbling and slipping over high rubble, he could not at first, because of the smoke, work out which building was the Central Post Office. He wondered if perhaps he had arrived at the wrong street, surely he had. But then he saw the symbol of the post horn above the portico and beneath it the flames. He was calm then, he was calm when he climbed up the scorching entrance steps. He was calm even when he began to shove his great weight against the locked entrance doors. He took hold of the door handles which burnt his hands. When he kicked and shrieked at the stubborn doors, he was no longer calm, not any more. And he began to wail then, he began to curse that thoughtless God in his heaven and to repudiate him with ever more savage and appropriate sentences. And then he was pulled and tugged away from the entrance by policemen, choking in the cruel heat.

And then he just stood. He stood still from a distance. Just watching, looking at the burning post office. Expressionless.

On I toiled, chipboard square after chipboard square, placing them gently into Irva's waiting hands as soon as I was out in the street again. And with each new square appearing Irva began to smile more and more. And the smile grew into a quiet laugh and the laugh grew into a giggling. And now each time I arrived with a new square there was Irva, giggling away, delighted at each new saved fraction of her city. And I too began laughing with her, together we, in hysterics now, were unable to stop ourselves from cackling in our plasticine triumph, as more and more of the city was safe.

Irva placed each part of the rescued centre of our city on the top of boxes until the trestle tables were free to be moved. The legs of the tables were easy, but the table surfaces had to be slid down the stairs and splinters cut into my fingers. But still I laughed, we laughed, we couldn't stop ourselves.

Once the tables were erected again, Irva began to put the puzzle of Entralla together.

Jonas Lutt would stop that afternoon and help anyone who asked for it, he even attended to those who did not call for him or even perhaps did not really require his attentions. He made himself useful, pulling away small boulders of masonry, alerting other men to places his strength could not reach alone. He attempted to comfort the tearful, he thought about nothing other than those poor scarecrow people around him. He gave a little boy his jacket and would perhaps have undressed himself entirely if that would have been of use. He helped other men tugging out the heavy, swollen corpse of a fat man who had died crushed in his bath. He saw a man dancing a waltz with the body of his dead daughter, calling out, 'I've found my daughter! I've found my daughter!' He saw rubble both sides of a street, no houses left at all, and in between a stilled and lonely trolley bus.

And it was only later, when he saw an elderly couple holding tight to each other that he began to shake. Delayed reaction, that's what it was. And it was only then that he remembered what he had seen when the flames of the Central Post Office had finally been extinguished.

We spent the entire day, quietly working on, our joyful cackling ignited again by the slightest thing, recovering the city of Entralla from its trauma. About us people made such noise it started our hands shaking, and we had to keep our hands steady then, it was most important. And then finally with the buildings back in the correct places, we allowed ourselves a little rest, while back inside our home Mother's room had slouched into the kitchen, and the whole house was lifting slowly up from the street, threatening to fall backwards. We'd have to jump up a little to reach our entrance step. But we didn't care then, not then, by then it was finished: a whole city in a street. How we laughed.

Jonas Lutt, seeing that elderly couple holding fast to each other, suddenly remembered that he had been one of the first to enter the Central Post Office on Napoleon Street. And suddenly he was able to remember quite clearly what it was that he had seen. Postman Kurt Laudus, who had once been a possible marriage candidate for Mother, who was a friend of mine from Café Louis, was buried under a fraction of the ceiling, but some of him was still visible, his face, for example, which was already bruised, even before the earthquake had happened, smashed by Louis in a jealous fit. Aged Grandfather, the postmaster, lay still and rigid in his office, with a strange grimace on his face, with his mouth open, with his clenched teeth showing, in an expression that would have suited an animal better than a human. And then Jonas saw, on the floor, burnt post office workers. From one of the steaming pockets a gloved fireman was able to pull out a post office personnel card which said on it, 'Marta Rena Stroud'. On the face of another body a small patch of unburned skin remained on which could be seen a roughly circular patch of black dirt, but perhaps it was not dirt but a rude fly perched there, but looking closely Jonas Lutt was able to see that that was not a patch of dirt or a fly at all, but actually a mole, which somehow curiously resembled the shape of a city far away in the Netherlands, a mole just like the one our mother had on her cheek, coincidentally in exactly the same place too. That was what Jonas Lutt remembered as he saw that old couple holding each other in front of him. He shook then with all his nerves as if an aftershock was being experienced in his person alone. He shook and trembled and quivered and could not steady himself. He would shake like this for three days and nights. He could not stop it. Some kind man gave him a bottle of brandy but as he brought it to his lips he was unable to stop himself from shaking it all over the street. Some kind woman tried to hug him but then she began to shake also and had to let go. He shook himself then in small, shaking, mechanical steps all the way to Veber Street. On his way, oblivious, he passed signs saying 'Do not enter this street – epidemic threatened', or, 'Ottila's hospital now re-opened', or 'Looters will be shot', but on Jonas shook, onwards to Veber Street.

Other people were in Veber Street by then trying to clear away the debris. He would not help them. He sat on an upright metal-framed plastic seat that had been flung from some house or other. The chair jiggled up and down beneath him. And then he saw our little city, and then he saw us. And he shook his heavy way down the street, and then we learnt about Mother, who, before that moment, we had not even thought of once, and then we stopped laughing and Jonas Lutt passed his shaking onto us.

'Mother!' 'Mother!' 'Mother!' 'Mother!' 'Mummy!' 'Mummy!'

That first night, we huddled and shook together in a makeshift home, not far from our old home, because Irva could not bear to leave the plasticine city. Jonas made this home for us from a canvas and old coats and jumpers. We sat on chairs which had once belonged to Miss Stott. Who could sleep, we wondered, with all that noise about the city, the great clatter of people saving other people? Seek out the sleepers, kick them awake, there should be no comfort, not until things begin to make sense again, because suddenly, within a few minutes, sense had been capsized, suddenly we lived in a nonsense city without electricity or water with thousands upon thousands of smashed homes and people, and we wondered: is this really our city? They should change all the names. Broken Street. Fallen Street. Bits and Pieces Street. Too Late for Help Street. No People Street. Upside-down Square.

People called out into the night: 'Where's our home? Where has it gone to? Give us back our home.' And I, close by our plasticine city, thought, 'Here it is, here it is.'

On the ninth day after the earthquake, we huddled around a radio, like the rest of surviving Entralla, to hear the wonderful news that even now a survivor had been found buried beneath the rubble of Trinity Square. A hospital porter named Alvy Phipps. That same day, when it was officially proclaimed that anyone left beneath the rubble must now be dead, we listened to a speech by Ambras Cetts – our acting mayor – which we would, in time, learn by heart.

It is the saddest, most savage, heart-gutting of a city that could ever be contemplated. So many of our people have lost

175

their lives. We remaining will never be the same again. But we have no time to lick our wounds, to comfort ourselves. We must forget for now all our very real tragedies and turn our minds to rebuilding at once. If there is rubble in our hearts, rubble that can never be cleared away by a million bulldozers, we must ignore it for now. In the next year alone I calculate that 2 million square metres will have to be built. There are around two thousand historic buildings in the earthquake zone, they must be rebuilt not torn down, we must resurrect our city even as we resurrect ourselves. I call on all the wealthy nations of the world, to be united in the one effort. To pull together with all your skills, to make Entralla rise again from its bloodied ground.

In those humpbacked days, we became used to the people of Veber Street gathering around the plasticine city and, silently, watching it. Whilst all about them was destruction something was giving them a little hope. It was as if the model was capable of pulling back time, so that as they watched it, if only for an instant, they could see themselves believing that everything was all right still, that nothing had happened. 'Don't come too close!' Irva always instructed, 'Stay back now! Step back!' They pointed here and there – 'Look the library isn't burning,' or, 'Look the Opera House is still standing,' or, and this from Jonas Lutt, 'I can see the Central Post Office, I can see it how I wish to see it.' Miniature things do move people.

The news of the plasticine city on Veber Street spread and soon people came from the neighbouring streets to view it. But amongst those people were some who were not so happy with our work, who crowded noisily around it, pointing too closely and said in loud, unhappy voices: 'That's not right, that shouldn't be there, take it out, take it out!' Why indeed should they stand quietly and regard upright buildings when their mother or father, wife or husband, son or daughter had been murdered inside such places? 'The city,' they said, 'no longer looks like that, this plasticine city is full of lies.' How they wished to smash the city with their bare fists, or feel it give way under their heavy boots; to pulp it even more than our city had been pulped. They considered that they could place all their heartbreak and misery onto the plasticine city; the plasticine could have their agony, they didn't want it. And some of those people pointing out various buildings that had been crushed or burnt or both, actually did lean forwards and seize them with their dusty hands, pulling the structures clear from the table, pinching them between thumbs and forefingers and replacing them in squashed and unrecognisable lumps. But they would not be happy with the removal of just one or two sacrificed locations, they began to get an appetite for crushing plasticine – anyone can do it, the substance gives such little resistance. They wanted our city to resemble yet another piece of the ugly and the broken; such things as we had at that time all over our city.

At first it was only Jonas and I who protected the city amid Irva's howls. Then the people of Veber Street who had known us and had lived just by us for nearly thirty years, and had heard of Mother and Grandfather's death, began to protect it too. They stood around the city, forming a barrier. Our neighbours said: 'Come on now, they're just children really, two girls who've never understood very much, it's not their fault, and their mother's just died, be reasonable, leave it alone, it's a plaything, it's all they have.' But the others called back: 'We've lost our mothers/fathers/children/friends too, that plaything offends us, we don't like it, we want it gone.' And the noises were getting louder and louder, the shrieks of the defenders, the shrieks of the attackers, and we were terrified that a riot would break out, for plasticine cannot stand up to riots. But it was because of this great noise that someone alerted the police, and the police did come and eventually dispersed the crowd. And it was perhaps because of those policemen that slowly the rest of the city began to hear of the plasticine replica.

Rumours of it spread about the smashed Entralla. Rumours whispered down tilted chimneys and through burst windows.

Rumours scattered down every broken street and square. Rumours along Napoleon Street. Rumours up the Paulus Boulevard. Rumours into the roofless cathedral swooping about it. Yes, these impossible rumours tumbled through every slanted doorway; into every twisted room; into every Entrallan that still moved. And some people said that it was a miracle; and others simply a story; and others still that it was a lie. And then, finally, someone must have told a priest called Father Hoppin.

Interlude 3

Supper

Tectonic House, Television Tower, Le Grand Lubatkin

For the final interlude of this tour our distinguished visitors have been given the opportunity to decide for themselves. There are many restaurants throughout Entralla, some catering to specific world cuisines for those foreign visitors of ours whose stomachs, unlike the rest of their bodies, are perhaps not prepared to travel. We have restaurants serving Italian, Thai, American, Chinese, Spanish, Polish, Japanese and Indian dishes, so that even in

Tectonic House

*Entralla foreign stomachs of those nationalities may be allowed to
feel at home. However, I would like to recommend three restaurants
which range across the spectrum of pricing from the extremely
cheap to the monstrously expensive. These recommendations may
of course be ignored, but all three of these eateries have been happy
to offer a 10 per cent reduction for those people seen clutching, the
perhaps by now slightly dog-eared,* Alva & Irva, the Twins who
Saved a City. *But whichever restaurant is chosen, or perhaps none
at all – in which case there are various supermarkets for the self-
caterer – I would like to take this opportunity to urge our visitors
to enjoy a digestif or a final coffee at Café Louis on Market Square.
It is the perfect place to end twenty-four hours in Entralla.*

TECTONIC HOUSE
Napoleon Street 112   Open 12:00–23:30   Tel. 316 34 26

*Tectonic House, with its glass brick roof (repaired), used to be an
indoor flower market, but the flowers, lacking water and buyers,
faded and died during the earthquake period. The International
Red Cross, people trained in misery, set up one of their many
centres here. In this building names of the deceased were published, and also photographs of the nameless dead. Soon people
arriving in their sorry states would be provided with water and
coffee and food also, until, over time, the building became the
cheap restaurant it is today and was renamed Tectonic House.*

    *The walls of the ground-floor rooms of Tectonic House are dec-
orated with a vast list of names, some fifteen thousand, skilfully
painted in black, of those people who lost their lives in the earthquake. A few names, of the more influential citizens, are painted
in red – for example, Rinas Holt, our former mayor; Constantin
Brack, the famous sculptor; and Mircas Grett, postmaster gen-
eral. Among this list of names in the less exceptional black it is
possible to pick out Krina Stott, tailor; Kersty Plint, single parent;
Artur, Clura, Piter, Prina Misons, toy shop owners and their*

*progeny; and even post office workers Marta Stroud, Kurt Laudus,
Victor Urdin and Dallia Dapps.*

*There is no menu, only one dish is available here at a time,
generally soup, served with our local black bread. But it is good
wholesome soup and excellent strong-tasting bread. This is a
subsidised restaurant and you will find your soup and bread will
cost you roughly US$ 1.50. Backpackers extremely welcome.*

TELEVISION TOWER RESTAURANT,
Bank Street 5–7. Open 12:00–23:00   Tel. 316 66 66

*The Television Tower is remarkably a survivor of the Great
Entralla Earthquake. Few people frequent the Television Tower's
famous revolving restaurant for its food. It specialises in averagely
priced fare (a typical meal costing around US$ 10–15), of which*

Television Tower

but little skill has gone into its preparation. Nor do people ascend the lift here for the excellence of the service found at the top. But despite the service, despite the food, this is a popular place; for Entrallans positively do visit the top of the Television Tower for the view. As their meal is consumed our people look down on Entralla and try to work out exactly where their homes fit in amongst that maze of buildings. At night, with Lubatkin's Fortress floodlit, it is an extremely pleasant sight.

The proprietor of this restaurant has pointed out to me that since the Plasticine Galleries were opened in the Art Museum of Entralla, he has suffered a fall in customers.

LE GRAND LUBATKIN
Pijus Street 2   Open 20:00–24:00   Tel. 316 21 23

Even with a 10 per cent reduction, the Grand Lubatkin restaurant is really only for our most well-heeled visitors. Subtly furnished, with exceptionally attentive service, only the elite of Entralla have

Le Grand Lubatkin

been privileged enough to taste its culinary masterpieces: red pepper mousse with aubergine caviar, crab flan in a parsley emulsion, red mullet cooked with aniseed and home-made pasta, coddled eggs with asparagus, terrine of rabbit with stuffed artichokes. Reservations are generally necessary, and the restaurant is often booked up for months in advance, but every effort will be made to squeeze in visitors carrying Alva & Irva, the Twins who Saved a City, but, to aid success, discreet donations to the maitre d' are welcome and advised.

The secret behind the success of this gastronomic palace is to be found in its French chef, Monsieur Daniel Arlin; indeed the restaurant serves only French food (which every Frenchman will tell you is the greatest of all the world's cuisines). Monsieur Arlin's mother, the stunningly beautiful Isubel Blukk, however, was an Entrallan, who left our city for a school outing to the capital of France and, having been spotted in a café on the banks of the River Seine, became the lover and then the wife of a Parisian chef and never returned home again. Their son spent much of his childhood in the kitchens of the Ambassadeurs Restaurant, inside the grand Hotel de Crillon on the Place de la Concorde, while Isubel in a fetching uniform changed sheets and dusted rooms. The boy was equally fascinated by his father's profession and his mother's stories – stories of her old home so far away – which she used to tell him at night just before he went to sleep. He vowed one day to visit that home, and he was true to his word. The result: the Grand Lubatkin.

Bon appetit.

Part Four

ENTRALLA & ENTRALLLA

Two Sisters of Pult Street
Were Once Given the Keys to Our City

Pult Street

Pult Street, of predominantly red-brick buildings, is at first glance an unremarkable street of Entralla. Accessed by trolley bus 12, the ninth stop from Cathedral Square, it was on this street that the twins passed their remaining years in our city. No. 42 Pult Street was their home and is now of course the residence of the Alva and Irva Dapps Museum, open from 12:00 to 23:00 – so late a closing

42 Pult Street

time to ensure our distinguished foreign visitors a chance to visit it at the end of their tour. The museum contains such treasures as Linas Dapps' fatal stamp collection, many of Postmaster Grett's matchstick models, Dallia Dapps' book on baby care, numerous press cuttings and photographs, among these the pre-autopsy photographs of Alva Dapps revealing her extensive tattoo. But the greatest exhibit of the museum is to be found taking up much of the second floor. Here you will find a room from 27 Veber Street, but this is no reconstruction. No. 27 Veber Street remained in its listing state for some fifteen years. It has been demolished now, but before demolition Entrallan conservators and archaeologists carefully removed the attic from the house and with it all its contents – its piles of notebooks, so many drawings and photographs of Entrallan buildings dotted around the walls, with plasticine fingerprints all over them – and reassembled this room and its objects carefully within the museum on Pult Street. Guided tours. Gift shop. Wheelchair access.

★   ★   ★

The fire on People Street, begun by the earthquake, destroyed the entire contents of our Central Library, lost in that tragic blaze were many hundreds of precious books and manuscripts, many irreplaceable items of great civic importance. After the fire was out, after about a week, when the ruins had cooled sufficiently, Ambras Cetts – in his capacity as acting mayor – visited the wretched place. What he saw there resembled the ugly crumbs of some merciless war: there were single walls perversely still standing quite black now with sorrowful holes where windows once were, but nothing of the insides. Mostly there was just black, toxic space, not even metal had survived, it too had melted under the savage heat. The former position of the Central Library was only distinguishable because somehow its marble entrance steps, cracked and blackened, were still there, though now they lead nowhere. If you climbed those fifteen steps they would take you only to a drop of five metres or more. That was all that remained of the library – a great open space, populated only by the ashes and dark fragments of so much defeated knowledge.

Our city had become a gallery of extraordinary sights, it had been singled out as the backdrop to sensational photographs. A few days after the quake whole families, if they were still whole, would set out to peruse the devastation and to have themselves pictured for the sake of future generations in front of this amazingly twisted mass or that dramatically bent street.

The Opera House was perhaps the most popular. The people loved to be photographed standing outside it so that the full extent of the damage could be seen; or inside it just beneath the main rotunda, surrounded by twelve bent Corinthian columns. The earthquake had undressed the Opera House. Gaunt and cold, it stood a shell of a building, lacking bricks and marble.

After the earthquake some loquacious people didn't talk for weeks, and, conversely, the taciturn suddenly found they could not be quiet. Amongst that latter group was Efrim Alt, the administrator of the Opera House. How he cried when the Opera House shook off its clothes, how he clambered up and down those buckled grand Baroque staircases in distress calculating the damage. He wanted the singers to come, to bring their music. Their music, he would swear to it, would be able to replace the dome, would sweep the carpets, would remove all the dust and debris on the seven hundred and eighty-two seats, would reunite the chandeliers and launch them back up to the ceiling. Perhaps just one aria would do all the work, but the singers never came. Efrim Alt found a kind of solace in the props store: an old-fashioned, wind-up gramophone. He placed the gramophone on the rubble-filled stage and let the sounds of scratched records of *Turandot, Tristran and Isolde, Don Giovanni* leak out into the empty, roofless vastness.

It was Father Hoppin who was the first to understand the healing power of plasticine. He had seen all those lonely souls wandering around piles of rubble or staring into empty plots. People did a lot of walking in those weeks after the earthquake, strange nocturnal perambulations into the city's darkness and into their own. People set out on these walks from their new temporary places of habitation to visit their old homes, they were out on those nights looking for their pasts. People had died once upon a time in those plots where cranes now loitered. How the priest longed to comfort his shattered people, if only he could find a way.

It began gradually enough. Jonas Lutt, whose house, like ours, was marked for demolition, and who found himself looking for Mother as much as we did, came to live with us in Grandfather's old home, bringing all his things, his chest of drawers, his photograph albums. Slowly Jonas and I moved the city into the back of his lorry, stacking it up, he tied the trestle tables down, Irva watching us all the while, wincing every now and then, tutting and muttering to herself, naming the streets and squares and how they joined onto one another. He helped Irva up into the lorry, onto the seat next to his, where Mother had once sat; he belted her in, she didn't complain. He drove so slowly, while all the time Irva watched him with suspicion. The journey took us about seven hours, before the earthquake it would have taken perhaps twenty minutes, and Irva was unable to relax the whole time. All the real houses around her, all the sunken streets we were passing meant nothing to her; to her those places she saw through Jonas's windscreen were of scant reality. There was only one place for her, only one place to live. It was dark when we reached Pult Street. Jonas suggested we move the city in the morning, Irva wouldn't hear of it. We all slept the night in the lorry.

As we moved it in the next day, Irva, conducting our work, would demand every now and then that we pass her a certain box. She'd lift the lid to check the contents, she'd sniff at them and smile. She paid no attention to Grandfather's house, showed no recognition of having been there before. I do not believe she had any comprehension of it at all, she could focus only on plasticine. When Jonas and I had finished moving in the city, she smiled at the great lorry driver and even held his hand. She'd often hold his hand in the future. And so would I.

Some people had seen us carefully moving the city in and later they knocked on the door and asked to be shown our plasticine miracle. With Jonas's encouragement, Irva seemed not to mind, as long as they didn't come too close, as long as they didn't get in her way.

Our visitors sat around Central Entralla in Grandfather's sitting room, quietly involved with the business of grieving. Mostly our visitors just sat mutely, but sometimes they pointed here and there commenting, for example: 'I remember when People Street looked like that,' or, 'Do you know I had completely forgotten that that building used to be on Arsenal Street,' or, 'How may years do you think before the Opera House will be reopened?' Then our neighbours began to come without invitation, bringing drink and food, at all hours of the day and night and they would never be turned away. More and more people came to know of the plasticine city, those residents of Pult Street telling their friends and relatives, and soon the house swelled with callers, with people looking at their lives. They understand them more when they are in miniature.

Calamity can have the consolation of bringing people together. In the past people had kept their happiness and their misery to themselves, but suddenly they found they were eager to share these. It became a custom to light candles around the city, the same candles that are found in our churches, prayer candles, candles for the departed souls of our city. And with these tiny flames lighting up the city at night, the congested house became a little dangerous, and once a woman singed her hair, so we had to begin rationing the visitors, and then queues started to form outside in Pult Street. Soon we were forced to refuse all visitors to the plasticine city. They had got so close, they had leant forward and touched even though I begged them not to (why must people always touch, why is it always such a need with them), they had barged about, and ignored us when we asked for some peace. It was on the day that someone accidentally was jogged and a small part of Liccu Street was dented that Irva, spitting fury, had Jonas Lutt push everyone out. There would be no more visitors, and when people knocked on the front door and shouted at us through the letter box we learnt not to get excited and to wait for the voices and the knocks to go away. But they'd always come back again, after a while, because there was such a passion for plasticine in those days.

And then one morning Father Hoppin came and knocked calmly. 'I have a suggestion,' he said. 'Would you please let me come inside.' He sounded reasonable so we let him in. Father Hoppin, as thin as he was serious, was one of the priests from the Renaissance church of Saint Onne's, perhaps the third or fourth oldest building in Entralla. His mother happened to live on Pult Street, he had brought the candles when everybody else brought food and drink. Yes, we recognised him, what was his suggestion? He wondered whether it would be possible to move the plasticine city to his church, he would place it in the crypt, people could visit it there without disturbing us. The priest explained that there would always be someone present to watch over the city, that the prayer candles would always be kept at a suitable distance. What did we think?

No.

Under no circumstances.

Utterly impossible.

Quite unthinkable.

'The city is ours,' Irva protested, 'we made it, for us, it belongs to us.' 'Yes,' said Father Hoppin, 'but consider please that you made the city in more peaceful days, when the laws of ownership were very clear, now everyone must help each other in whatever way they can. You,' he continued, 'have a chance to help, to provide comfort, and that is a great gift, surely you will not deny the good people that comfort?' Irva yelled, 'But it's ours, it's ours!' He said, 'Surely, my children, it is everyone's; the city, after all, belongs to no one person.' Irva said, 'You're ripping it from us!' He said, 'No, merely requesting that it be moved to a more public space where more people might marvel at your extraordinary achievement.' I said, 'But it's so delicate, it would take so little for it to be ruined.' He said, 'I promise you every effort will be made to ensure its safety, but consider please that plasticine is not a substance that was made to last so very long, consider that in a short time it will have dried out and become brittle, it will be cracked and dirty, and then it will be too late for anyone to learn just what it is that you have created, please give your work the recognition it deserves.'

Irva didn't speak then. She was beginning to wonder where she would live if the city were moved. Her head between her knees, she was trying to calm herself. At last, she looked up. She reached out, took hold of one of my hands and of one of Jonas's and made the following slow and serious announcement, 'The city shall be moved.' She nodded. She smiled. She continued. 'But wherever it goes . . . I go too.' It was incomprehensible for her to spend any time away from it. The city could be moved anywhere, perhaps even out of our country, perhaps continents away, that was unimportant to her, what mattered was that she remained by it. She would live, next to the city, inside the crypt of Saint Onne's Church. She announced her intention to the priest, and in those unhappy days when so many newly homeless people lived inside the undamaged churches of Entralla, he found no reason to argue with her. And I would come too? 'Of course,' she said, 'obviously.' And so Jonas Lutt lifted Irva up once more. And so the central portion of the plasticine city was moved to the crypt of Saint Onne's Church. Seven hearses arrived the next day through the ruptured streets to fetch it. And later Jonas came in his lorry with the rest of the city, with all the boxes, which were piled up in a disused chapel in the corner of the crypt. Soon there were candles again, all around the city. Soon there were rows of kneelers and fifty or more people quietly fingering rosaries. On occasions a priest delivered his prayers over the city and sometimes the choir would even sing around it. Father Hoppin told us that the plasticine model brought hope to our people. It was all rubble outside the crypt, but at least there was hope inside, people adored the miniature city, it was an exhibit that spoke of their own lives, and they found solace there. And Irva, smiling, felt a part of something, felt that she belonged, more than ever before. People would come and talk to us, every type of person, old ones, children, nuns, lovers, men in suits, they would ask us about our city, and always then it was Irva who answered.

They were so interested in us during those days. How they noticed us! How they looked at us and marvelled: two long women in the darkness of the crypt, sitting quietly on a pew together, surrounded by boxes, illuminated by the candles around a plasticine metropolis. Perhaps some of them even wondered if we were saints. Perhaps Irva was beginning to believe she was a saint, she could certainly hold a solemn pose for the longest time and she never once pulled her hand away when an old woman wished to kiss it. Sometimes we'd sit quietly with Jonas in between us, his hands around our shoulders, gently stroking.

About a month after the plasticine city had taken up its new residence in Saint Onne's crypt, a man in a perfectly fitting suit, woke us early one morning. We crawled out from under ur blankets. He told us in pronounced whispers, to add to the import of his message, that our mayor, Ambras Cetts, had been informed of the existence of the plasticine city and had even visited the crypt of Saint Onne's, two days ago. We had noticed him; did the man talking to us now, think that we wouldn't notice this new visitor wearing chains of gold around his neck? Ambras Cetts, we were told, had been very impressed with what he had seen. 'Yes?' Irva yawned. (She was so used to impressed people by then.) Ambras Cetts had even insisted the Reconstruction Committee visit the city. So that was the party of men, we realised, in perfectly fitting suits. 'Well?' The model, the man told us, was potentially most useful in their work, particularly since so many maps and photographs of the city had been destroyed in the People Street fire. The plasticine city had answered many questions for them, and it was useful in arguing against the international officials when they wanted only to put simple cheap buildings up where once great architecture had stood. With the help of the plasticine city, with the international officials actually viewing the entire city as it once was, our politicians would perhaps make major progress. Something as simple, our visitor informed us in his ponderous whispers, as plasticine was swaying grown men. It had become their blueprint for rebuilding the city, it had become indispensable to them. 'In a way the plasticine model had,' he said, 'saved our city.' And Irva nodded with equal seriousness, she entirely believed him.

The man wanted to ask permission to have the city moved again. To a lighter place where it could be more easily viewed. It had all been thought through, he said, we had only to agree. It would be taken to one of the conference rooms in the City Hall, the public would no longer be allowed to visit it. It was called to higher things, reconstruction architects and politicians wanted it now. Besides, it would be better looked after, the man whispered, in the City Hall. 'But,' Irva said, 'do you want all of the city or only the central part?' He didn't understand. She showed him the other boxes. 'What's in those boxes?,' he asked. 'Entralla,' she said, and opened a box so he could see. The man looked shocked, no longer in whispers he said, 'But all the boxes . . . It's enormous . . . All Entralla?' 'No,' I said, 'we didn't finish, we were unable to finish because of the earthquake.' The man scratched his head. He said, 'It won't fit in any of the conference rooms.' Irva said, 'No, most probably it won't, it's very big, you see, very big.'

Over the next few days different men in suits came to visit Saint Onne's and to measure the boxes and to do sums and finally they said that they had found a place in which the whole city could be fitted. A warehouse, in Outer Entralla. And so the city was moved once more. This time in army trucks. And we were moved with it.

So the dust sheets of my days were pulled away, Irva wound me up with encouragement and her new-found confidence, she shuffled me unsteadily back to plasticine construction. We slotted the city together. No one else was permitted to help. It took us nearly two weeks. Their calculations had been faulty, they had to keep extending the large table (which was really several large tables bolted together) they had built entirely for our city – that table which we slept under in army sleeping bags at night. 'More?' they kept asking us. 'Yes, more,' we'd say. 'More. More.'

To see it in its entirety! Laid out in its completeness! All plasticine Entralla! Each chipboard square by chipboard square, slowly expanding. Only then did we truly understood the enormity of our work, only then could we understand the size of Entralla, the weight of it. And when the official people came to see it they gasped. Had we really done all this by ourselves, we had of course, no one else, don't you believe us? 'But why?' they asked, 'Why had we?' I told them, with shrugs, 'Maybe because we were lonely.' And we had to admit that it was incomplete. And that it was impossible to finish now of course.

Then we met Ambras Cetts, who was the man, unintentionally perhaps, who had killed our father. I was going to tell him, but instead we both just sat, smiling, nervous. This was our mayor, our mayor was talking to us, to Irva and to me! 'Excellent work,' he told us. 'Very useful,' he said. 'True patriots,' he said. 'Goodbye,' he said.

We never once replied to any of his comments.

We were to become a story for the digestion of the Entrallan populace. We were, with our plasticine city, to be pushed forward as an example of the Entrallan spirit. We were to be made a fuss of. They took photographs of us standing near the city, and on one occasion Ambras Cetts came to stand in between us and smiled his smile which made us forgive him almost instantly, even for Father's death. (We're taller than Ambras Cetts, we measured him, one hundred and seventy-two centimetres, how small he looked in those photographs with Irva and me either side of him.) They published articles about us. 'ALVA AND IRVA, TRUE CITIZENS OF ENTRALLA.' One said, 'PLASTICINE TWINS SAVE CITY.' 'How ridiculous!' we cackled, 'Some people will probably think we're made of plasticine!' They wrote how useful our work was in recovering Entralla. They made up strange stories about how each and every building was accurately measured, about how Grandfather and Mother had helped us, about how Father had died trying to save people in an old earthquake years back. One article even said: 'Michelangelo with his marble, Rembrandt with his oils, Alva and Irva with their plasticine.' They made huge posters which they stuck on giant billboards. Between a man on his horse in a cowboy hat advertising cigarettes and a nearly naked woman with a great waterfall of blonde hair standing in a sunflower field advertising shampoo, could be found Alva and Irva advertising hope. With the caption: 'IF THEY CAN BUILD IT SO CAN WE.' The North scars on our foreheads, we noticed, had been airbrushed out.

There was much talk in those days, and many arguments, about whether the actual city should be carefully reconstructed as it once was or whether the past should be forgotten and a new fresher city be made in its place. Mostly, people wanted the old Entralla back, and the designs put forward which gave the damaged parts of the city exact gridded streets with exact squares were quietly put aside. Many new buildings were to be built of course but mostly in the outer circles of Entralla and certainly never in the old town, which was to be carefully rebuilt in its former beauty (except for the Paulus Boulevard; Paulus suffered most of all, ancient, sophisticated buildings would in the future look onto duplicate blocks). Enlarged photographs of the plasticine old town were placed on stands throughout the actual old town. One article said that we, the Dapps twins, had inspired it to be rebuilt, because from our model it was easy to see just how wonderful the old town used to be. And everyone, or so it seemed to us, was talking about the glorious architecture of the old town, when before, when they had seen it every day, they had barely thought of it at all. Ambras Cetts presented us with two plaques on which were keys. We were given the keys of the city of Entralla, and with them came something called the 'freedom of Entralla', which we had thought all along was already ours.

They let the people of Entralla come and see the plasticine city. There were large queues around the warehouse, but they weren't allowed to come too close, they weren't allowed to touch. They put ropes around the city, and only we were allowed to go under those ropes. They fixed red velvet curtains all around the edge of the model. Often when all the people came to see the city we would be underneath the massive tables, hidden from sight by the velvet curtains, listening to all those many people talking about plasticine Entralla (talking about themselves, the geography of their lives). We whispered to each other, trying not to cackle too loudly, occasionally peeping out through the curtain to see all the different types of the shoes of the people of Entralla. We remember once someone from a place called Wibb Street complained because Wibb Street hadn't been built with plasticine; it was as if his home didn't exist. But it did exist, we hadn't reached it, it was too far out, that was all. On that day there was also an art critic from one of the newspapers, and he said: 'Such is the way with all art. All art, my dear fellow from Wibb Street, can never be totally completed, only, in the end, abandoned unfinished.'

And that was how we passed our days mostly, under the table of our city. And when the people had gone we'd creep out of our hiding place and look all over the city and see where we thought the plasticine needed repairing. And sometimes Jonas would come and stay with us. But the truth could not be hidden from us. Slowly the city was drying out, losing the sharpness of its colours, we kept putting fresh plasticine over the cracks but the cracks kept coming back, whole squares would have to be replaced, and we couldn't get to the centre of Entralla without dismantling the table which the entire city was standing on, and they wouldn't let us do that, and we saw how grey with dust Lubatkin's Fortress had become. And as the city declined, as it shrivelled and creased, so, it seemed to me, Irva declined, she shrivelled and creased too. The worse the city's state became the less Irva was interested in repairing it, she was content to watch me looking after it but unwilling to help. She looked at the cracks, at the gathering dust, at the faded colours, at the dehydrated suburbs, with increasingly detached looks, and she preferred to sleep now when people came to visit the warehouse. She no longer cared about their footwear.

And as the city's illness increased, as it wrinkled in its old age, it seemed to me from under our table that there were fewer and fewer shoes to watch. Slowly the number of people visiting the city was declining, until in the end there were only ten or so people a day. And the other people who worked in the warehouse said it didn't seem worth opening it to the public any more, because the public in those days had lost their passion for plasticine.

Our brief and local fame was over.

Afterwards, when the warehouse was closed to visitors, I would leave Irva sleeping under the table, and walk about the city and see that the large advertising posters of us were hardly anywhere any more and when I did see them often they would have been graffitied over. Our teeth had been blackened out or naked breasts had been drawn over us and once I even saw drawings of men's penises right next to our faces. I defaced one poster myself, I tip-toed up in the train station, I added two arrows, pointing upwards, and two 'N's.

And then all the posters were covered up. And if there were any articles about us now they were mostly unkind articles that said we were backward, that Irva was practically feral, that we had deliberately cut ourselves off from people even as we were amongst them. One article stated, 'It is a true sign of the insignificance of our city that whilst other cities have artists like Michelangelo who work with marble, or Rembrandt who paints in oils, we must have two introverted women who play with a substance designed for infant usage: plasticine.'

I knew why all this was. It was because it was taking so long to reconstruct Entralla, a year already and still so much of it was rubble. People wanted to forget about the earthquake, they wanted to cheat themselves with lies about it never having happened. They never looked up at the cranes and they cursed the plasticine city. They wanted to get on with their lives, they wanted to forget us.

And they were probably right. It was probably time for the city to die. Jonas said we must forget it, that it had made us ill and that, until we'd forgotten it, we would not recover. Irva and I moved back into Grandfather's house in Pult Street. Irva didn't say very much. After we'd been there a few days she never mentioned the city again.

About the actual city, they fixed the Central Post Office. They put Corinthian pillars at the front, taken from another building that had been more completely ruined, they put metal counters inside. It barely resembled our old post office at all, but at least the old steps were still there. What a confusion the postal service was in in those days. Which address exists, which doesn't? Postmen, people who before had known their individual parts of the city so well, would come back asking where such and such a street was, they couldn't find it anywhere. A new postmaster came from a nearby town. He was a man who had no understanding or love for Entralla, to him it was always the mound of rubble the earthquake had made of it.

I was frequently confused about the city. I'd stop still in the street sometimes, just stalled there, looking about, not really knowing where I was going. Nobody recognised me as I wandered Entralla, I would have to have been with Irva to be recognised. There is nothing particularly exceptional about a twin alone without her sister, even if she does have a North sign upon her forehead, or a map hidden beneath her clothes.

So we just stayed in Grandfather's house mostly. Jonas did try to get us to come with him and he did look after us well, and occasionally set Irva talking again, but we couldn't find the energy to go anywhere any more, nor barely to look out of the window, not when everything out there was such a mess, not when we recognised so little of it, not when it made no sense. Endless days, surviving on Grandfather's money and Jonas's rent, days without purpose. And always we felt so tired.

We would never have survived without Jonas. He was always there, holding our hands, brushing our hair, cleaning up after us. He even bought plasticine for Irva when she asked for it again.

I returned to my old vague dreams of travelling and began to spend hours in Grandfather's bathroom flopped naked in front of the mirror. I talked again of other countries and other far-away customs. Sometimes Irva would let me walk her up and down the street, once Jonas even carried her piggy-back all the way up Prospect Hill, from the fortress she looked out but she didn't seem to see anything.

And then she started building miniature 27 Veber Streets.

27 Veber Streets. One after the other. When we told her it was time to eat she'd shuffle into the kitchen, shovel the meal down her, mutter, 'Thank you', and as quickly as she could, shuffle out again. I saw her on so many occasions staring so seriously at those models of 27 Veber Street, as if she were wondering how to get inside. Jonas and I took her to Veber Street once, wondering if that would help. I do not know whether it was because our home was boarded up or because of the 'DANGER' signs written about it, but for whatever reason Irva didn't seem to recognise our old home

at all. And she carried on, day after day, building more and more 27 Veber Streets. She even started to place them together, she made streets of them and then, one day, she embarked on her final city of plasticine.

★ ★ ★

ON THE USEFULNESS OF PLASTICINE BUILDINGS. 3: Searching. *Even now I cannot regard the third and final exhibit in Gallery 24 without upset, for it is upsetting let there be no doubt about that. It is a city that can only conjure negative feelings. It is an evil, mean, limited place. If this city were to have inhabitants, they would surely one and all be shifty, suspicious people filled with disquiet and malevolence. They would range from petty thieves to habitual murderers. If there were any children there, they would be secretive and awkward, they would have imaginary friends who would constantly get the better of them. It is a city composed of hurt and self-neglect. On a first sighting you may assume that I am a man subject to gross exaggerations, for it will likely seem to you that there is nothing particularly upsetting about this model. It is set out, plausibly enough, like many another city; it has patterns of streets, squares, boulevards and parks – it is in fact based upon the city of Entralla. But as your studying becomes more thorough, you will see that this entire city consists only of one building, endlessly repeated. On this city's version of Cathedral Square there is no cathedral, but only, once again, that same house, always the same size no matter what building it has usurped, and in the place of the bell tower and baptistery again you see that same house. On the top of this city's Prospect Hill there is no Lubatkin's Tower but only that same house. That same house in every road, street, square. You may initially have thought this was a curious city, amusing possibly, but you'll soon find the repetition makes you nervous, you demand that something be different, but it never is, you see, not there. It is that same note played over and over again, the same note as you look through those streets rising in volume, until it fails to amuse you, it nauseates you, it disgusts you. In an effort to make your thoughts consider something new, you perhaps begin to wonder why this city was built, you begin to think of the person who built it. You see her now, all alone, day after day, constructing the same house over and over again. How long, you wonder now, did it take to construct? Eight months. Eight whole months with nothing but that same house day after day, week after week, month after month. Her dreams, you suppose, and you suppose correctly, must have been visited by that same house, by multitudes, armies, empires of that same house, with nothing to disturb it, to break the distressing monotony of that awful same-ness, because as she runs in her nightdress in her nightmares down ill lit streets, she would come across in her horrifying trauma a vast and endless maze consisting solely of that same house.*

★ ★ ★

After there were hundreds of 27 Veber Streets (each less accurate than the first) to be found all over the house; after she'd completed her mock-city; after we couldn't move for 27 Veber Streets, a new and final stage came over Irva. She started building tiny cubes, endless lines of cubes perfectly formed, all the same size.

'What is it, Irva? What are you trying to tell us?' But by then she had stopped speaking. She just pointed to those cubes, or would earnestly hold them up to us. Later she'd come in to see Jonas or me in our separate rooms, or together in his, and would give us a cube, 'Thank you, Irva,' we'd always say, 'thank you very much.' She'd smile, kiss us both and leave the room. When those cubes had grown dust Irva would take them away again, she'd crush them and replace them with new ones. And it was only later, much later, that I understood that Irva's cubes represented a single room. She was building again and again a single solitary room. This woman who built cities, this woman who it seemed to me could construct whole worlds, this woman had now reduced herself to a single, tiny, cube-shaped chamber.

And then she stopped building altogether.

And then she sat still all day, quite useless, and wouldn't be encouraged.

'Hello, Irva, come back wherever you are.'

The doctors visited her, they said 'nervous exhaustion' and gave her some pills. The pills seemed to make no difference, she still sat there, looking but not seeing. I built again for her, I built miniature cathedrals and opera houses, I built fortresses and post offices, I built homes. She held them in her hands a while until her wrists became tired and they fell to the floor. She was lost inside herself, and I couldn't get her out. I showed her photographs, a copy of Mother's book on baby care, Grandfather's matchstick models, I showed her my map, I placed her hands upon my map but they only slipped off again. 'Come back, Irva, come back, please. Where've you gone? Where is it that you are now?'

I dressed her everyday, I heaved her with Jonas's help into a wheelchair and walked her about the recovering city, sometimes people stared at us. She slept on our walks mostly. I'd take her into Café Louis, repaired now, I'd get an Entralla bun and mix it in a bowl with a little milk, and spoon it into her. It seemed to me that she smiled sometimes. Was she finding a way out, was she trying to get back? I washed her body, her frail, lonely body, my sister body, but I am not certain that she ever knew that it was me that was touching it. 'Irva, hello. Hello, Irva.' Or, as if she were a child, 'How's Irva today?' 'Where's Irva today?' But she had gone.

All along she had never really wanted to come out, she'd peeped out for a while, it's true, but in the end, she'd gone back inside. Deep within. She's probably happiest there.

I go looking for her sometimes. And sometimes I think these little sentences: The world is on my skin. The world was once swallowed by my sister. There are stars on the ceiling of our train station. Outside the train station, up in the night, are the actual stars. We kept a city with us in our old house. Us, in the world, Irva and me, standing on a sphere.

I'm going on a journey. I've been sitting here in Grandfather's house in Pult Street, writing this history of my sister and me, so I can get it out. So it can be left behind, for I shan't be taking it, or her, with me. I'm unburdening myself. I'm shedding history. But it must be kept, for it is a history of Entralla, just like that of Grand Duke Lubatkin, however humble. Or perhaps it is only the history of a street, or even only of a single house in that street. Or perhaps it is the history of a city, only of a city made of plasticine. And perhaps, like all those other faded cities, like Knossos or Persepolis or Timgad, it's right that, even though the city has fallen into ruin, still some history of it remains.

Sometimes, when I climb stairs, it takes me a while to get my breath back. I know why it is, it's because I'm tired. Whilst I write this history, I have to keep taking breaks. I haven't been well. I need a change. I shall be leaving soon, and most likely I shan't be coming back. I want to be somewhere else, I want to be anywhere, anywhere that is not 42 Pult Street, anywhere that is not Entralla. I want to see streets I don't recognise. I want to see people I've never seen before. I want everything to be new. I hate anything familiar, I hate what I see everyday through these eyes. I loathe it, anywhere else is wonderful to me, no matter how soiled, simply because it is not here. That's all I crave: somewhere that is not here. If only to glimpse it so briefly, if only between blinks. That would do.

A New Statue for Our City

The new statue for our city is of twin sisters. At their feet is a model in miniature of the central portion of our city. The sculptor has caught them, he has re-created Alva and Irva (if perhaps a little idealised). Quick, I told him, when at last he had finished his work, quick, cast them in bronze, the clay's too vulnerable, someone might knock them over, someone might feel the urge to press their fingers deep into their clay flesh. And now they will last.

I returned to Entralla some twelve years ago, to a very different Entralla than I had known in my youth. At times I was hard-pressed to recognise it at all. Fortunately the old tower remains; some things, after all, do not change. But all the same this was home, I had come home. If indeed there was a home anywhere for me now.

In Canada, years ago, I had rowed and lost touch with my brother. I was amazed how little time it can take to lose a family. For a long while I never thought of home, sometimes though I'd catch myself wondering about Alva, about whether she thought of me, about whether she was perhaps still waiting for me, spending lonely afternoons looking at the ceiling of Entralla's Central Train Station. Then, after years of ignoring my past, more and more often, for no particular reason and quite involuntarily, I took to sitting on my own in cafés mumbling to myself, trying to recall my own language. But so much I had forgotten. I began to write endless little notes of only a few sentences, of instances of my childhood that I was able still to recall, and once I had a few of those memories on paper many more came rushing back to me, and with those memories how I felt I had rediscovered my home, I could feel it again. And with each memory returned I felt more

myself. I spent more and more time alone, remembering. In the
end it seemed increasingly obvious to me that I must in fact
return home. I told people at work that I'd be gone a week, ten
days perhaps, that was twelve years ago.

I shall not leave Entralla again.

For a month I lived in the International World Hotel until
finally I had the courage to admit to myself that I was not going
back. Then I rented a small apartment near my mother's old house
on Dismas Street. My mother had died six years before and I'd
never known, I'd never felt that she had died, I've no idea what I
was doing the moment of her death. The pain I now feel because
of her death is so surprising to me because of its ferocity. I wake
up calling for her. A grown man of fifty so terrified of the dark,
calling for his mother! I've become one more of those sombre faces
in the crowds, full of personal and obscure sadness. My sister
married, she has two children, I look at them, I look at my niece
and nephew, I touch them, I think: what an achievement. It is not,
after all, so easy to lose a family.

I bore people with unspectacular memories of my distant
places, I begin my sentences with 'That reminds me of when I was
living in . . . Of course in such and such a place things are very
different . . . Did I tell you about my journey to . . .'

To begin with I just walked Entralla. I saw the cathedral, still
then with its temporary roof of tin, I walked the Paulus Boule-
vard and People Street and could not recognise them. I saw Bread
Square, site of my father's death but also of my childhood, I
walked and I tried to remember. I had hoped that one day on these
visits I would come across Alva or her sister. I allowed myself to
imagine Alva asking to marry me, I felt I could picture the scene
so accurately. But I did not make any true attempt to find her then.
When I did, after nearly two months and longing for company, I
searched the telephone book; there were many hundreds of Dapps
listed there of course. I rang any with the initial D for Dallia and
though I spoke to several Dallia Dapps none was the mother of my
friends. Then I rang any A. Dapps and any I. Dapps, again with

the same result. I could not find them anywhere. I returned to Veber Street to discover their house boarded up, leaning at a dangerous angle. There are still many houses like this about the outer streets of Entralla, waiting to be tugged down or rebuilt, a fraction alive but mostly dead. Every now and then, I hear reports on the radio of adventurous children who climb inside them, and then these houses shut like a trap, they collapse, as if they'd been waiting for those children all along.

I looked at the register of the earthquake dead in Tectonic House, which in my youth had been a flower market. I found a Dallia Dapps among the lists but no Alva or Irva Dapps. A young woman there, not I think originally from our city, asked me whom I was searching for. I told her I had been away for a long time, I was looking for my friends, I told her the names, she shrugged, she apologised, but at least, she said, they were not killed in the earthquake. As I was leaving, an older woman who had been mopping the floor stopped me. Was it the twins I was looking for? she asked. Yes, I said surprised, you know them? No, she said, she never actually knew them, but they were true and great Entrallans. But she had said 'were'. The twins were dead? Yes, she told me, several years ago. Several years ago.

And in that instant my future life seemed to shrink before me to contain in its cast of characters only a single, nervous August Hirkus. But there would be room enough, there would be so much room in fact, for the memory of twins. I suddenly realised quite how much I missed them.

I spent the next two weeks patching together Alva and Irva's lives. The information could, incredibly, be found in the New Public Library on People Street. In the small but growing archive section. I scrolled through the microfiches of old newspapers. People had written articles about my old friends, many articles. Whilst I had been growing increasingly unspectacular thousands of miles away, Alva and Irva were being written about.

I learnt of the transient fame of their plasticine city. In the old newspapers (newspapers collected only since the earthquake) were so many stories of so many lives, but then I scrolled down little history after little history, and, quite suddenly, there they were. Alva and Irva. I had found them again.

The facts are simple enough. On a particular April morning, Alva Dapps climbed aboard trolley bus 7 with a suitcase. As she travelled from Pult Street, towards the centre of the city, en route to Terminus Road and the train station, there was a brief spasm inside her and her heart ceased to beat. The time of death, the coroner's report states, was around seven thirty a.m. On that particular morning the trolley bus driver, who was new to his situation, and who was called Andrius Chapin, was not willing to stop the trolley bus despite the fact that he had a dead body inside it. He continued on his normal route, prepared only to make the brief regular stops that the trolley bus company had stipulated, ignoring the protestations of the passengers. This event made, for a very brief time, international news and for a far longer period national news. The reason it appeared in the international news was because some simple Entrallan believed that since Alva was a celebrated person of our city, she would be known throughout the rest of the world, and that therefore all the journalists of the globe would be interested in her demise and so he sent the story off to international news stations. It turned out that foreign newspapers were interested in Alva's death, but not because of who she was but only because of the manner of her death. Her death, it seems, spoke of the increasingly growing terror people all over the world have of losing their jobs, and what such fear is actually capable of doing to people on a day-to-day level. How frightened we have all become – even in little-known and distant cities such as Entralla.

One local journalist suggested that this final journey of Alva's on the trolley bus was like the victory laps that athletes like to take after they have run a race. And perhaps, the journalist wondered, if he had been in the trolley bus that day with dead Alva and had looked through the window, he might have seen the buildings in the centre of our city actually bowing to her slumped form, in gratitude for her life. Such stories are, of course, to be dismissed as mere fancy. But every now and then, I have witnessed Entrallans pausing in their days when a trolley bus slips off its overhead lines and the driver has to put on gloves and with a special rubber hoop realign the cables – such actions, it seems, remind them of the death of Alva.

On the afternoon of her death, when the police knocked on the door of 42 Pult Street to inform the surviving twin of her loss, no one came to answer. A police car waited in the street for someone to return. When, finally, a lorry drove up that night, the occupant of which possessed keys to the house, the police discovered Irva inside, in her bed. Quite still. Her eyes and mouth open. The coroner's report estimated that Irva had died between half past seven and eight o'clock that morning.

The name of the lorry driver, used several times in the Entrallan newspapers, a name I had not heard of before, was Jonas Simas Lutt. Mr Lutt, I discovered in the telephone book, still lived in that house on Pult Street (where I too now live – in the attic space at the top of the museum). I telephoned him. He remembered my name. We agreed to meet, but where I wondered. The telephone went silent for a while, then he said Café Louis in Market Square, that was a good spot, though he later confessed that he'd never been there himself, only that one of the twins had occasionally mentioned it.

Jonas Lutt is a big man, with slicked-back hair, usually dressed in commonplace jeans and a T-shirt. I would recognise him, he said, by the T-shirt he was wearing of Rouen Cathedral. Jonas and I have become friends. We often go together to that Market Square café with its sullen proprietor. And it was on one of those occasions that he boasted to me that he, Jonas Lutt, an ordinary-looking man from Entralla, a man so ordinary in his features that he would disappear in any crowd, seen as simply a perfectly *plausible, unexceptional urban male, that he, this long-distance lorry driver, had an extraordinary secret. For years this man of small conspicuousness had been making love to two women. Not every night, for sure, only on occasions, but nevertheless it had still occurred. A surprising fact perhaps, given the blandness of the confessor, but hardly revolutionary; such behaviour is certainly not unheard of (even in a Catholic country, perhaps particularly in a Catholic country). But this man, since he first lived in his current address on Pult Street, had been making love to twins, one at a time. One night Alva. The next Irva. How extraordinary Entralla's version of Casanova is, a tall and tubby lorry driver. No one seeing him walking down a street would suspect this man's past. He made love to Irva, he made love to Alva (he made love to a map of the world). Until they became too ill. For comfort.*

Jonas has told me that when Alva set out with a suitcase that morning he thinks she knew what the outcome would be. He thinks that Alva understood that in separating herself from Irva she would cause their deaths. They had been struggling with living, he said, for so long.

I asked Jonas what had happened to the plasticine city. He didn't know, he hadn't heard about it for years. Probably, he thought, it was destroyed. We decided to find out. The most obvious place to start of course was the place it had last been seen. We journeyed to the warehouse on the outskirts of Entralla, on Illtud Street. There was a rusting padlock on its entrance doors. We couldn't undo the padlock, we had no saw with us, and just as Jonas was suggesting he should go to fetch one, I gave a final push at the doors and they both, through old age and rot, collapsed into the warehouse and I went tumbling in after them. And there it was. After all that time. The plasticine Entralla. Defaced by dirt and dust, walked over by spiders, with great webs spanning whole sectors of our city, with dead flies and even a dead bird or two upon the cracked surface. Perhaps it no longer really resembled Entralla, but all the same, here it was, the forgotten city.

At first we thought we might be the only people interested in the city but as we worked on it, carefully removing the dirt with tweezers and a slightly dampened cloth, filling in the major cracks, we began to wonder whether such a marvellous creation would not in fact be of considerable interest to many people. In the end we decided to write a letter to the former mayor, Ambras Cetts, who was living, we discovered, as a virtual recluse inside the International World Hotel, in fact just two floors above the room where I had so recently stayed. We tried not to put our hopes up. We waited. A week later a letter arrived, former mayor Cetts was delighted the city still existed, but he assumed it must be terribly ruined. We sent him photographs. He decided to come and visit it, breaking his vow, since he had been diagnosed with cancer, never to leave the hotel again. He was frail and walked with a stick and a nurse. He wept when he saw it.

Then followed all the fuss; the photographers and journalists' visits to the city, the public's increasing demand that they should be allowed to see it too. Entralla was growing obsessed with its history of Alva and Irva. The photographic negative from which the posters of the twins had been made was eventually found, and more posters were printed. People began to buy plasticine, more and more. The Alva and Irva Museum opened in Pult Street. But it was decided that at all costs the miniature city must be preserved from too much disturbance. To appease the public, Lubatkin's Tower was carefully cut from the city and a cast was taken of it and from the cast many plastic fortresses were made, which were placed beneath small transparent plastic domes, and the domes were filled with liquid and small white plastic flakes. Plastic fortresses, souvenirs of our city. Five thousand were made. Five thousand were sold. A further ten thousand were made. When these too were quickly purchased, more and more were made, until the whole of Entralla became saturated with these